PUBLISH, *DON'T* PERISH!

4

ENOUGH IS ENOUGH

Jay B. Brodsky, MD

FOREWORD

I first met Jay B. Brodsky MD (Jay), the (now) sole author of "Publish, *Don't* Perish! #4 Enough is Enough" at Stanford in 1977. At the time he was a newly appointed assistant professor of Anesthesiology having recently been discharged (escaped) from serving in the US Army. Major Brodsky's only claim to fame during his two years of active-duty service was that he had been allowed to shake the hands of President Gerald Ford during the latter's visit to San Francisco. Why the Secret Service permitted that to happen remains a mystery, but you can be sure the President was happy to be released from Jay's clutch. Many of us were not so lucky. Jay didn't wash his hands for months after this momentous event with an otherwise forgettable President, and this might explain why he had not washed his hands after writing three previous editions of these also forgettable "Publish, *Don't* Perish!" books.

It was obvious from our first meeting that Jay was destined to become a famous academician (certainly in his own mind). His early seminal works included studying the hemodynamic effects of intranasal cocaine (1) and publishing a very personal case report on the treatment of intraoperative penile tumescence (2). However, it was his study on the effects of waste anesthetic gases on the survival and life of the semen in male anesthesiologists that attracted the most attention (3). Nobody had ever done that before, and nobody has been that foolish to attempt a similar study since then. This important scientific "breakthrough" got him an invitation on Good Morning America. There, in characteristic style he made the most of it but left everyone including the television interviewers completely bewildered. As an apparent result of this national televised performance, NIH support for anesthesia research plummeted throughout the country. Just to be clear, many people including surgeons and hospital administrators continue to be bewildered after any meeting with Jay.

As important as these papers and the many other contributions Jay has made to the medical literature, his most influential publication was on efficiency in the operating room (4). This frequently cited paper recommended counting "1-2", not the usual "1-2-3" before moving a patient. This maneuver results in saving one second with each patient move. Although Jay took credit for this idea, it was actually an observation he made working with orthopedic surgeons in our operating rooms. In the ortho OR counting beyond 2 was considered unnecessary, wasteful, and in many cases a challenge. This paper was the inspiration for the Publish, *Don't* Perish! series since it proved that almost any vague concept or simple idea could be published somewhere.

Those of you who have read any of the three previous books in the seemingly endless "Publish, *Don't* Perish!" series will perhaps recognize that I was reluctantly listed as an author in each of the three previous volumes. I tried, but I was regrettably unsuccessful in attempting to improve the quality and content of those books. When this 4th book was being planned, I was determined to extricate myself from this Sisyphean project. As you know Sisyphus was a king who annoyed the gods (read "physicians") with his trickery (read "Publish, *Don't* Perish!"). As a consequence, Sisyphus was condemned for eternity to roll a huge rock up a long steep hill and watch it roll back again only to repeat the process. There is a strong movement afoot to make Jay repeat this rock rolling venture as a punishment for his continuous production of these books. When I told Jay that I had enough of his futile attempts to increase the prestige of these books by listing me as a co-author, he put on a brave face and said he did not mind, but his disappointment was clearly evident. Like Sisyphus he will continue to carry on this unending literary disaster. Why he begged me to help him with the previous volumes is a mystery as my suggestions and comments were always ignored. For the sake of our friendship, I did reluctantly agree to continue my participation in the second and third volumes but like the readers, I was always disappointed by the final results. My attempts to rectify his ways for the sake of the few people who might actually buy and read these books were a failure. If you have purchased or attempted to read any of the previous volumes, you can see that I truly did fail. This book is like the others – a complete lack of literary finesse that could only see the light of day in the underworld of self-publishing.

However, some of you may find this volume amusing. Do not be upset. You are not alone. Based on the sales figures for the previous volumes, there are many others who may think as you do and appreciate the author's sarcastic humor. I, on the other hand wish that this madness will soon end. As the title states, let us hope that volume # 4 finally does mean that Enough is Enough!

1. Brodsky JB, Goldwyn RM: Hemodynamic effects of intranasal and I.V. cocaine. New England Journal of Medicine (1977) 296:1008
2. Welti RS, Brodsky JB: Treatment of intraoperative penile tumescence. Journal of Urology (1980) 124:925-926
3. Wyrobek AJ, Brodsky J, Gordon L, Moore DH, Watchmaker G, Cohen EN: Sperm studies in anesthesiologists. Anesthesiology (1981) 55:527-532
4. Brodsky JB: Cost savings in the operating room. Anesthesiology (1998) 88: 834

John G. Brock-Utne, MD, PhD
Stanford, CA, February 2021

PREFACE

The Publish. *Don't* Perish! series has praised the availability Internet resources to publish work that mainstream established journals reject. This book, the fourth of the series, continues to give examples of manuscripts that would never be accepted in a traditional medical journal, but would be published immediately by any one of hundreds of Internet journals.

A recent example emphasizes the value of these alternative journals. With all the current controversies during the COVID-19 crisis, it's logical to think that results of a randomized controlled trial to test whether face masks actually work would be important. Prior to the COVID crisis the Centers for Disease Control and Prevention (CDC) cited at least 10 published randomized controlled trials that showed "no significant reduction in influenza transmission with the use of face masks." Then came the COVID pandemic and the CDC changed its position on universal mask-wearing. The CDC, the World Health Organization (WHO), and politicians now want us to believe that coronavirus is transmitted differently than the common flu and other coronaviruses. Actually, a large-scale trial studied whether face masks protect against COVID spread was completed in Denmark in mid-2020. This study examined the effect of universal mask-wearing specifically against the spread of COVID-19. It involved 6,000 participants, with half of them wearing masks and the other half served as a control group and did not wear masks. The study was submitted for publication, and then rejected by three important established medical journals (New England Journal of Medicine (NEJM), Journal of the American Medical Association (JAMA), and Lancet). The Danish authors implied that these rejections were due to the study's 'controversial' results. One stated, "If its results were what the 'media-political-scientific complex' wanted it to show, that is, that masks work, it would have been published immediately." It was finally accepted and published on-line by another journal, the Annals of Internal Medicine (1). The report, in fact, did not find that wearing face mask protects the wearer from becoming infected with coronavirus. These findings of course contradicted the position of the CDC and Washington.

This example raises an important question. How many other scientific and academic studies covering controversial policy questions, many unresolved and currently involved in scientific debates, are censored because they don't fit the narrative of the politicians in power? What's next? What other *controversial* information is being suppressed?

This is where Internet journals can fill an important niche - publication of studies and ideas outside the mainstream. If influential journals like Lancet, NEJM, and JAMA refuse to publish your paper, the 'International', 'Global', or 'World' Journal of ------------ (fill in the blank) will gladly give your work a voice. The Danes could easily have published their study earlier on one of many Internet journals, and if they had done so it would have immediately made an impact. Perhaps your work has shown that fossil fuels are actually safe for the environment, or that being morbidly obese is actually advantageous to your health rather than harmful. Would Lancet or the NEJM publish your findings? Probably not. The main-stream media and journals and many of their peer reviewers are biased, and they will accept and publish only those papers that fit their agendas. Internet journals are different, they will publish anything you submit to them as long as you pay the publication fee. Yes, it can be expensive, but your message will be heard.

Don't let your study or discovery remain suppressed just because the findings are "politically incorrect", or your methodology was not performed in the accepted scientific manner. As highlighted in each of the previous 'Publish, *Don't* Perish!' books, you have the benefit of a vast array of Internet journals, magazines, and conferences each ready and anxious to publish your manuscript, so submit your correspondence, reviews, articles, and proceedings (commonly referred to as C.R.A.P.) to any one of them and share your work with us ….

1. Bundgaard H, et al. Effectiveness of Adding a Mask Recommendation to Other Public Health Measures to Prevent SARS-CoV-2 Infection in Danish Mask Wearers. A Randomized Controlled Trial. Annals Internal Medicine. (2020) Nov 18:M20-6817. doi: 10.7326/M20-6817.

Jay B. Brodsky, MD
Palo Alto, CA, February 2021

Disclaimer: The contents of each of the 'Publish, *Don't* Perish!' books, including this one, are intended as humorous works of fiction, and sometimes they actually are funny. Most of the names, characters, businesses, places, events, locales, and incidents are the products of the author's imagination and are used in a fictitious manner. Occasionally the name of a real politician or physician may appear, but only in the context of a recent newspaper article in which they were also named. Otherwise, any resemblance to actual living persons should be considered coincidental. These books, although discussing medical topics, are certainly not intended as a substitute for medical advice by the author (who is an anesthesiologist and has no knowledge of most of the medical conditions discussed).

CONTENTS

ACKNOWLEGEMENTS

THE COVID CRISIS

1. Smoking Kills Coronavirus

In a surprise announcement the COVID Task Force claimed cigarette smoking prevents coronavirus infection. Dr. Anthony Fauci said, "We've known for many years that cigarette smoke can destroy living tissue." Recent experimental evidence from China has shown that the novel coronavirus is remarkably susceptible to tobacco smoke (1). Although pipe and cigar smoke may reduce viral loads, subjects who smoked at least one pack of cigarettes each day had the lowest infection rates. Even individuals who became COVID+ had only minor symptoms. When asked about potential side-effects from smoking, Dr. Fauci hesitated. "I'm the world's expert on infectious disease," he modestly stated, "but I don't know anything about any other areas of medicine. I always base my recommendations on the science, and I'm told that scientific studies have repeatedly shown that tobacco smoke can kill. Nothing else I have recommended or that we have tried has been as effective in preventing COVID."

1. Li I, Too ME, Yu F. Cigarette smoke kills coronavirus. A novel approach to COVID prevention. R.J. Reynolds Ann Med Report (2021) 6:12-6

2. Competition Intensifies Between Chinese Labs

Following the overwhelming success of the Wuhan Institute of Virology releasing COVID-19 to the world, other Chinese laboratories are now working on creating newer, even deadlier diseases. Government research funding is competitive, so each laboratory is trying to develop their own deadlier pathogen. The Guangzhou Bacteriology Laboratory has produced a mutation in Yersinia pestis, the organism responsible for bubonic plague. A slight change to the bacteria's RNA now renders it totally immune to all currently known antibiotics. "We expect a lot of damage from this tried-and-true killer," Dr. Su Me the director of the institute proudly stated. "We have already infected fleas on cargo ships and airplanes, so like the coronavirus the plague will be widely distributed before anyone identifies the source." Not to be outdone, Dr. I. M. Wong of Chengdu Medical College claims his team has found the source of the Antonine Plague that ravaged the Roman empire in the Second Century. Until now the identity of this mass killer has remained a mystery. "Since nobody but us knows whether the culprit is a virus, bacterium, or even a prion, development of a vaccine or treatment strategy will be delayed. We can cause even more havoc than those incompetent Wuhan people accomplished with their puny virus." President Xi Jinping (below) expressed his country's pride by saying "China has always been about innovation and we now can justifiably claim to be the world's leader in producing pandemics."

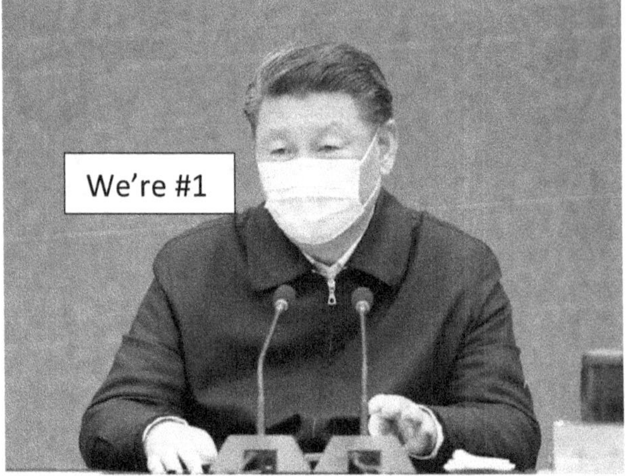

Figure. Supreme Leader Xi Jinping is proud of the role his country played in creating the COVID pandemic and says he plans to continue to work on destroying the world's economy.

3. COVID Vaccine Distribution List

In mid-December 2020 the entire world welcomed the wonderful news that several coronavirus vaccines were now available. Since initial supplies were limited, plans to administer vaccine to those at the highest risk were formulated. Unfortunately, no matter how you prioritize a distribution list, someone will always complain and feel cheated. For example, more than 100 selfish physicians at a prestigious medical center in the San Francisco Bay area (Ed note: not UCSF) held a raucous protest their famous university prioritizing other hospital workers to receive coronavirus vaccine ahead of residents and clinical fellows who were working directly with COVID+

patients. The protesters accused hospital leadership of allowing non-essential employees to be vaccinated first. They noted that only 7 medical residents and fellows were included in the first round of 3,900 vaccinations. "Health care heroes go to the back of the line!" chanted the doctors as they spilled out from the hospital into the plaza in front of the facility. They raised signs including "Front line workers need protection" and "Residents can die, too." When several hospital leaders stepped up to address them the angry crowd quieted down. "You got it all wrong," hospital president and CEO Donald Bentwhistle told the crowd. He explained that the vaccine distribution algorithm they used closely followed the federal government's guidelines. "Hospital administrators are essential leaders in the battle against COVID and therefore must be immunized first. It's a war, and like any other war, a heathy leadership is a priority for success." He continued, "We have 47 vice-presidents, and dozens of directors, managers, and assistants, and each and every one of them is essential. I still can't believe we actually vaccinated 7 resident physicians when the Vice-President for Fonts in Advertising and her 6 assistants were excluded from the first round. We have 1300 physician residents and fellows but only 47 vice-presidents. The loss of a single vice-president would be a disaster, while any residents can be immediately replaced. Of course, administrators must get the vaccine first." He cited federal government practice in which politicians also receive the vaccine before healthcare workers, residents of nursing homes, and the sick and elderly. Addressing the house-staff he continued, "Look at the fine example of Rep. Alexandra Occasional-Cortez (D-NY). She courageously went to the head of the line to get vaccinated early to demonstrate to her "at-risk" constituents that she needed to stay healthy in order to be there to represent their survivors. Your hospital leadership was inspired by AOC's example. So, don't be so selfish … get back to work and be patient, your turn will eventually come!"

Germany to Hold COVID Restriction Violators in Detention Centers

WS

German quarantine breakers to be held in refugee camps, detention centers

GERMANY

COVID jails: Germany clamps down on quarantine violators

4. Germany to Hold COVID Rule Breakers in Camps

Chancellor Angela Merkel announced today that Germany's worst COVID rule breakers will be held in what she affectionately called *'detention centers'* under new proposals being drawn up by a number of regional state governments. Figure. She claimed the move is needed by the Fatherland to stop the spread of the contagious mutant strain of the virus first detected in the UK last month. She said, "It's a modern Battle with Britain and this time we will succeed! We will *concentrate* all undesirables in special *camps*. We have more than 80 years of experience building and supporting these types of centers." Germany's regional governments have powers to hold people who flout lockdown requirements under the Aryan Disease Protection Act, first passed by the federal parliament in 1932. Current lockdown measures are due to expire on January 31, but Merkel told members of her Christian

Democratic Union party that the country still needs "eight to 10 weeks of hard measures". She reminded them that "the Reich wasn't built in a day".

Figure. A smiling Chancellor Merkel and regional leaders discuss plans for new detention centers to house rule breakers and other undesirables. Merkel envisions a bright future for Germany.

5. Americans Should Consider Wearing FOUR Face Masks

[News: January 28, 2021] Dr. Scott Segull, chair of Anesthesiology at Wake Forest Baptist Health in North Carolina told NBC News today that Americans should consider wearing *four* face masks if they want better protection against COVID-19. Just recently Dr. Fauci advised people to wear two masks, saying that it "makes common sense" that more than one layer will be more effective. However, soon after Fauci made his recommendations, researchers at Virginia Tech said that two face masks only provide 50-75% efficacy and that three masks should be worn to achieve almost 90% effectiveness. But according to Dr. Scott Segull even 3 masks are not enough. "If you put four masks on, it's better because there are more layers." Segull's advice was then criticized by a noted surgeon Jeffrey Bordon who said, "Two masks are already going too far. I can't breathe wearing just one mask during surgery." At this point orthopedic surgeon Dean Carradine interjected. "Four masks are only 90% effective. I did the math and 90% is not 100% effective." Carradine advised Americans to wear five masks for increased safety. His comments were echoed by YouTube fashion influencer Charles James. James asked "why concern yourself with trivial matters such as breathing when wearing multiple face coverings is so effective in delivering social media clout? The more face masks you wear the greater the number of fashion statements you can make. More masks will also allow you to display all of your favorite sports teams." Shortly after the NBC News interview Etsy sold out of the Scott Segull® Collection of four-layer face masks. Figure. Manufactures are working night and day to produce a five-layer Carradine® Collection face mask.

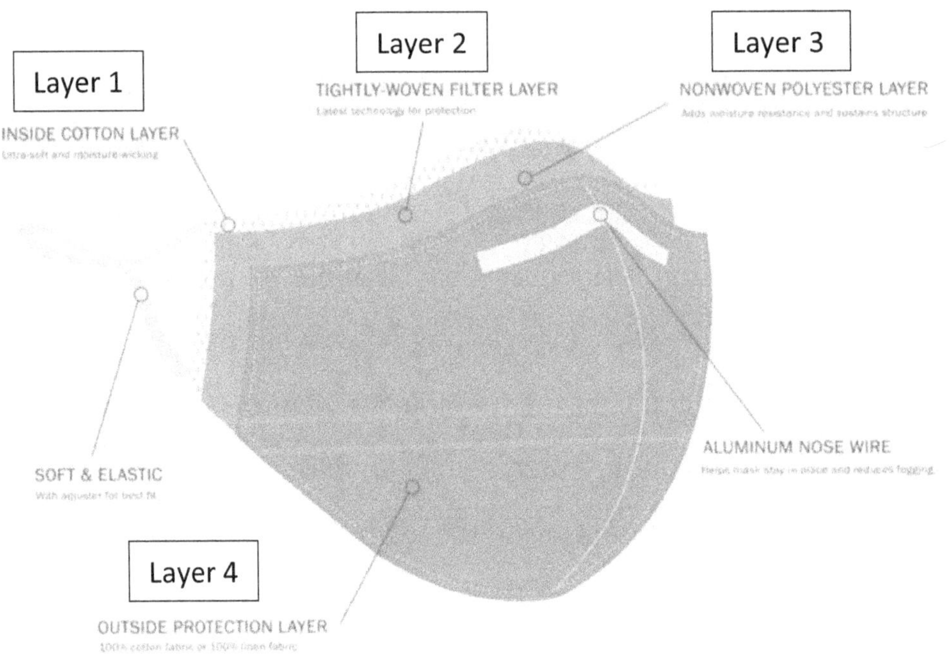

*Figure. The **Scott Segull® Collection of four-layer face masks makes** a fashion statement, while providing the wearer state-of-the-art protection from coronavirus.*

6. Maduro' Announces 'Miracle' Treatment for COVID-19

President Maduro proudly announces the development Venezuela's cure for COVID-19. To honor of his country's contribution to world health, he awarded himself the coveted Venezuelan Heroes Medal made from the last gold chain left in his country.

[News: Jan 26, 2021] Venezuela's President Nicolás Maduro has announced a cure for COVID-19. Maduro said the drug, *'carvativir'*, has been under testing for months. "Ten drops under the tongue every 4 hours and the miracle is done," he said. "It's a very powerful antiviral that neutralizes the coronavirus." He kept secret the name of the "brilliant Venezuelan mind" behind the discovery. He plans to distribute carvativir nationwide and to share it with other nations. That news was greeted with enthusiasm around the world. The WHO immediately nominated Madura for the Nobel Prize in Medicine. President Madura said, "carvativir will be made available to anyone living in or visiting our country. Only capitalistic pigs in the U.S.A. and Europe have a tiered system for distribution of vaccines and COVID treatments. Here in Venezuela everyone is equal."

7. Anal Swab Test for COVID

China, often the butt of jokes on their handling of the pandemic they created, is now applying a new approach for mass testing for COVID. The test involves inserting a swab one inch into the rectum, rotating it multiple times, and then removing it and sealing the swab in a container. Figure. Yang MiChian, a senior doctor from Beijing's People's Rectal Hospital #4 said the anal swab method can increase the detection rate of infected people because traces of virus remain longer in the anus than in the respiratory tract. Asymptomatic COVID+ patients can recover quickly and have no trace of the virus in their throat after 3 to 5 days. Compared to samples taken from the respiratory tract, the virus lasts longer in the digestive tract and excrement, especially after a meal of bats or pangolins. There are risks with the new test. One patient who underwent COVID testing said, "I had an anal test and then a throat swab immediately afterwards. To save money the nurse used the same new swab twice."

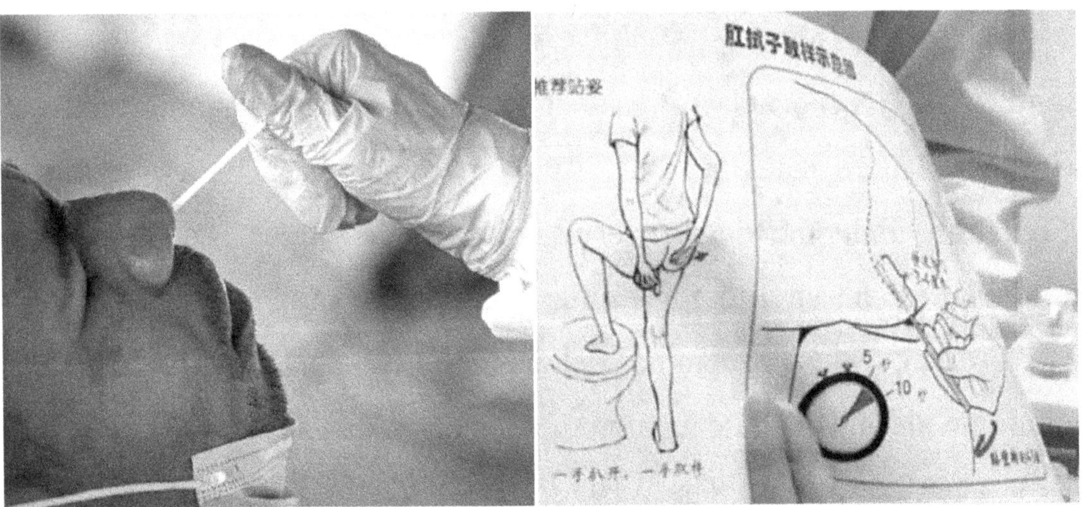

Figure. (left) The usual test for COVID is a nasal swab that many patients find uncomfortable. Instructions for the anal swab test are conveniently printed on rolls of toilet paper (right). Innovative Chinese scientists are using the anal swab to test men for both coronavirus and prostate disease.

HEALTH CARE

8. Insurance Company to Deny Services

These are difficult economic times for health insurance companies. The COVID pandemic has produced an overwhelming number of claims for hospital services, so many insurance companies have sought ways to reduce their expenses. NeverCare Healthcare, the administrators for our hospital's insurance carrier, Aetna, has just released the company's new rules for reimbursement. For example, any patient with a bleeding ulcer will no longer be eligible for surgical repair since the ulcer was present before the bleed occurred and thus is a 'pre-existing condition'. Likewise, permission for emergency surgery for a ruptured cerebral aneurysm will be denied. No admission to a hospital for a myocardial infarction will be allowed unless the patient had undergone physical therapy and exercises to improve coronary blood flow prior to the heart attack. Failure to have done so makes you ineligible for a bypass or stent. There is no admission to the ED for treatment following a traffic accident without prior pre-authorization. The list goes on and on. The only procedures that are guaranteed, of course, are sex-change gender transformation operations since "it's everyone's right, not privilege, to be who they want to be" according to NeverCare. The good news is full-term abortions will still be fully funded under the new guidelines. These improvements in healthcare policy were applauded by President Biden who believes they will unite the American people. They will be applied equally whether you are a racist older White man or a recently arrived undocumented immigrant. He noted that if a protestor is hurt during a riot in Portland or Philadelphia or other city, he, she, or them, will be treated to the full extent of their medical needs completely at government expense. Exceptions to this policy will be policemen and other first-responders who "don't belong in the midst of a social protest and therefore are held responsible if they are injured" according to Vice-President Harris.

9. Pregnancy Testing for ALL Women

Women undergoing general anesthesia and surgery during early pregnancy may have an increased risk of miscarriage, premature birth, low birth weight infants, and infant death. However, it remains controversial whether all women of child-bearing age should have a pregnancy test prior to elective surgery. The overall frequency of positive incidental preoperative pregnancy tests ranges from 0.34% to 2.4%. A report by the American Society of Anesthesiologists Task Force on Pre-anesthesia Evaluation allows hospitals to implement their own policies and practices with regard to preoperative pregnancy testing. Our hospital has had a requirement for a pregnancy test within 48 hours before surgery for all females between the ages of 15 and 55 years. The surgeon has the option of not ordering a test on anyone who has had a hysterectomy or has experienced menopause. Until recently we had also excluded transgender women assigned male at birth but who now identify as female. Our failure to apply the same rules for testing these women led the ACLU to file a challenge in court. "A woman is a woman, whether she has a '**Y**' chromosome or not!" the ACLU representative successfully argued. "Excluding these women from preoperative pregnancy testing demonstrates institutional bias and is unacceptable." So, we now require pregnancy testing on anyone who identifies as 'female'. We are happy to report that, to date, the incidence of positive preoperative pregnancy tests among the transgender female population has remained zero. No positive tests yet! Since this is the first survey of pregnancy testing among transgender female surgical patients we plan to submit and publish our results in an Internet medical journal. Given the success of our pregnancy screening initiative, we will now routinely perform prostate-specific antigen (PSA) testing on all transgender men assigned female at birth.

10. Avoid Surgery on Surgeon's Birthdays

A study in the British Medical Journal reported that patients who had emergency surgery on their surgeon's birthday had a higher risk of dying (1). The study, supported by a \$3 million grant from the NIH, analyzed data on nearly 981,000 emergency operations performed on Medicare beneficiaries by 48,000 surgeons between 2011-2014. In the 30 days after surgery death rates were 6.9% among the 0.2% of patients (N=1,962) whose procedures were performed on their surgeon's birthday and 5.6% among the other 99.8% patients (N=979,038), a difference of about 23%. The researchers weren't able to identify the mechanisms that led to the higher death rate, but they suggested that to be safe, patients might want to avoid surgery on their surgeon's birthday. Further analysis of the data yielded additional important information. Operations on Valentine's Day were dangerous if the surgeon was currently involved in a messy divorce. Operations on or the day following St. Patrick's Day by a surgeon of Irish descent were associated with even high complication rates. The mortality rate for patients (N=1) whose surgeon Dr. Paddy McGuinness was celebrating his birthday on Saint Patrick's Day and whose wife had just left him was an incredible 100%! The authors concluded that before deciding on a date for surgery patients should ask their surgeon (a) the date of his birthday, (b) his family's ethnic background, and (c) the current status of his marriage or romantic relationship. They consider this information essential. The same research team now plans to use a new \$5 million NIH grant to determine if operations performed with unsterile, contaminated instruments account for more surgical site infections than when clean equipment is used.

1. Kato H, et al: Patient mortality after surgery on the surgeon's birthday: observational study. BMJ (2020) 371 doi: https://doi.org/10.1136/bmj.m4381 (Published 10 December 2020)

11. Chiropractors Seek to Adjust Their Practice

Spinal manipulation or 'chiropractic adjustment' is a procedure in which a non-physician chiropractor uses his hands or small instruments to apply a controlled, sudden force to a spinal joint. The goal is to improve spinal motion and the body's physical function. Spinal manipulation may relieve certain types of back pain, neck pain, and other musculoskeletal symptoms, but there is no scientific evidence that chiropractic adjustment can restore, treat, or maintain, health. Despite this, the National Association of Reliable Chiropractor Organizations (NARCO) has demanded that California license chiropractors to practice as fully trained medical specialists. "We go to school, we learn about muscles and bones and other body things, so we should be able to treat all medical conditions just like real doctors," a NARCO spokesman stated. "There is a bias against us just because our low school grades prevented us from being accepted into a medical or osteopathy school. Many of us come from diverse backgrounds, and on that basis alone we should be granted the same privileges as physicians." The California Board of Medical Licensing, which is always concerned about any form of bias, agreed. Chiropractors will now be allowed to treat the whole spectrum of medical illnesses including infections, cardiovascular and pulmonary problems, and malignancies. They have been cautioned to be gentle with spinal and neck manipulations in patients with metastatic disease to the bones. "What is *metastatic disease?*" the NARCO spokesman asked. Henceforth, chiropractors will be able to see any patient with any medical problem who seeks a spinal adjustment as a means for treating their condition, whatever that condition is. Upon hearing the Board's decision, other alternative health care groups including 'Holistic Medicine For All', 'United Shamans for Change', and 'Witchcraft for Informed Californians' have applied for equal consideration. "If chiropractors are licensed as legitimate health care professionals, so should we".

12. Healthcare Providers are Not the Same

Advanced practice nurses often represent themselves as being interchangeable with physicians. There is no doubt that certified registered nurse anesthetists (CRNAs) play a critical role in patient care. But they do not possess the same training or experience as a physician anesthesiologist. A recent op-ed article claimed that physician anesthesiologist supervision of CRNAs is "burdensome" and "unnecessary". This may be true in some situations. Why buy a luxury car when you can get to the same destination driving a Yugo? Why order a steak at a restaurant when you can satisfy your hunger with plain beans? Just as a Yugo costs one-tenth

the price of an Audi or Mercedes, medical services should be available at different costs? A board-certified surgeon may charge $10,000 to perform an appendectomy, while an advanced practice surgeon's nursing assistant can probably perform the same simple procedure safely for $5,000; even a medical student could operate and charge less money. But what if you are having a complex operation and/or have multiple medical co-morbidities? Would you want your neurosurgeon or cardiac surgeon to be replaced by a nurse or medical student, even if they charged half or one-fifth to operate? Health care providers are not equal and for complex operation a physician anesthesiologist is a better choice than a less expensive CRNA or anesthesia-extender. We think the decision should be up to you. It's your choice … and your life.

MEDICAL PRACTICE

13.   Inexpensive Treatment of Worm Infestations

Intestinal worm infestation is a global health problem. Soil-transmitted helminth (STH) worms affect billions of people worldwide, causing considerable morbidity and suffering. Intestinal worm infestations are widely prevalent in tropical and subtropical countries and occur especially in areas of poverty and poor sanitation. According to the World Health Organization (WHO), globally there are as many as 1.4 billion cases of Ascariasis (roundworms), 1.0 billion cases of Trichuriasis (whip worms) and 1.3 billion cases of hookworm infestation. An inexpensive universal treatment for STH would have immense benefit. During our weekly meetings at a local dive bar, the editors of Publish, *Don't* Perish! noted that a dead worm was present at the bottom of tequila bottles. Following a literature search we discovered that the worm is not in tequila but in a similar drink called mezcal, and it is actually not a worm but a moth larva. Nevertheless, based on our observation that something that looked like a worm was dead at the bottom of a bottle of alcohol, we performed the following study. Empty containers were filled with different liquids; tap water, carbonated water, soda, tea, aquavit, mezcal, or cachaca. A live worm was placed in each container. The following day the worm was still alive in the water, tea and soda bottles. However, the worm was definitely dead in the aquavit, mezcal, and cachaca bottles. This controlled scientific experiment proved to us that alcohol kills worms. Dr. Tedros Adhanom Ghebreyesus, head of the WHO was very impressed. Unfortunately, he and his family have been cursed with worms for years and nothing they've previously tried has helped. Dr. Tedros and WHO now recommend drinking two shots of alcohol three times a day in regions where worms are endemic. His insights have been noted by the Nobel Prize committee and Dr. Tedros is now being considered for a dual Nobel Prize in Medicine for his work with both COVID and worms. Cachaca, produced in Brazil from sugarcane, is the least expensive of the drinks tested. Its low cost and devasting effect on STH worms make it the ideal treatment for worm infestations in the developing world. We recommend a good aquavit for more affluent Scandinavians. In fact, an enterprising Norwegian, Ole Drunk, has produced an aquavit he calls N.M.W. ('No More Worms'). Ole claims that an advantage of following WHO's guidelines is that everyone can now be happy three times a day. If there is a serious worm infestation Ole recommends doubling the dose. He says that this will lead to even more happiness and more dead worms.

14. Crisis Nurse Called to Start Intravenous Line

Our nurses insert intravenous (IV) lines in patients scheduled for surgery. One doesn't have to have attended medical school or have any advanced training to place an IV. It is a relatively simple skill that requires a little practice to master. For some reason our nurses are reluctant to use an IV larger than a small 22-gauge catheter, no matter the size of the patient's veins. Recently, patient MRN #1323456 was scheduled for major surgery. Nurse Nancy I. Deere RN planned to start his IV and draw blood for studies. Despite several attempts she failed. She then called for an ultrasound (US) to identify any hidden veins that might be accessed. Even using the US she still failed to successfully start an IV. At this point, now desperate, she called the crisis nurse for help. "He's a difficult stick" nurse Deere informed the crisis nurse who was known for her ability to start an IV on even the most challenging patient. Unfortunately, even the experienced crisis nurse failed after several attempts. Just then anesthesia resident Dr. Donald Odom arrived to see his patient. "What's the problem?" Odom asked. "He's impossible" both nurses cried. "Let me have a look. "I think I might be able to find a decent vein." Figure.

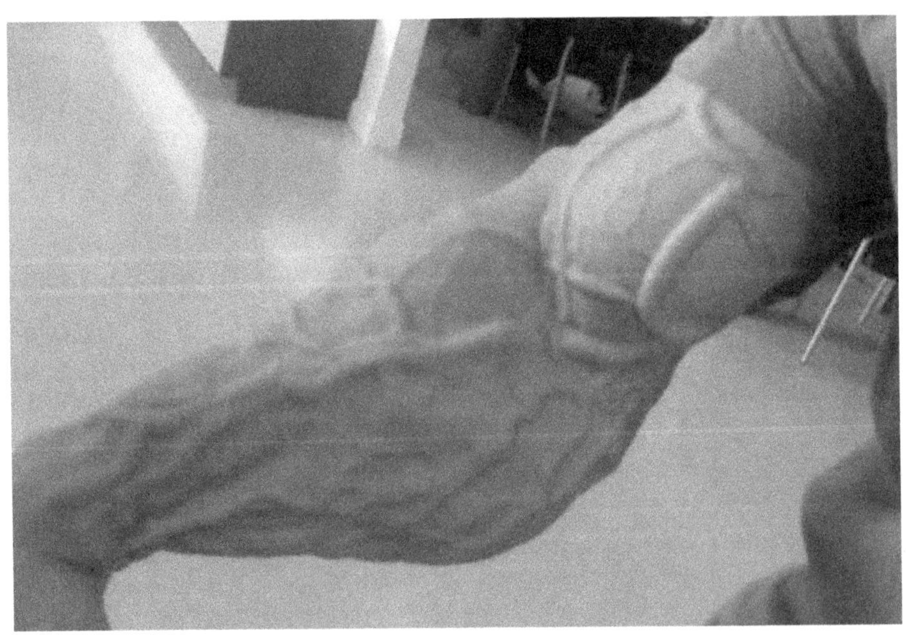

15.   Hospital to Serve Red Wine

Studies have demonstrated positive link between moderate red wine drinking and good health. Red wine has antioxidant, anti-inflammatory, and lipid-regulating effects. It is a rich source of resveratrol, a natural antioxidant in the skin of grapes. Although there are other antioxidant-rich foods including fruits, nuts, and vegetables, red wine is preferred by most non-vegetarians. Red wine lowers the risk of cardio-vascular disease and reduces blood pressure. It acts as a probiotic boosting healthy gut bacteria. It decreases the risks of type-2 diabetes. Resveratrol may also help prevent vision loss and reduces the risk of certain cancers. Resveratrol can protect against secondary brain damage after a stroke or central nervous system injury. People who drink between 2–7 glasses of red wine each week have lower levels of depression. Researchers found an increased risk of dementia in people who abstained from drinking wine. Clearly red wine is a miracle drug. If another drug with so many positive health benefits were available, it would be recommended to everyone. So why haven't hospitals taken advantage of red wine's positive properties? They now have. Our Health & Well-Being Committee recommends that red wine be served throughout the hospital. Meal trays for patients will include cheap wines and their insurance companies will be charged the usual 2000% markup. Since many healthcare workers experience depression and burnout on their job, red wine will be served in the hospital cafeteria. Nurses, physicians and other hospital employees will be allowed two glasses of wine with each meal, with more if you work with orthopedic surgeons. The executive dining room will continue to serve exclusive, expensive French wines. Given the positive health benefits of red wine, CEO Donald Bentwhistle has mandated that all Administrators consume a minimum of ½ bottle of wine with each meal. Since drinking red wine helps people live longer Mr. Bentwhistle hopes to not have to replace his drinking buddies as often.

16. Fecal Donations Level the Playing Field

The current economic crisis has resulted in record numbers of unemployed men and women. For years men have had the opportunity to earn extra money by donating their sperm to sperm banks. These banks purchase, store, and sell human semen to women for the purpose of achieving a pregnancy other than by a sexual partner. Sperm donors are usually paid between $50 and $125 for each acceptable sample. Unfortunately, for obvious reasons, the millions of women now out of work cannot serve as sperm donors. Recently feces have become an untapped monetary resource for both men and women. OpenBiomme, a nonprofit stool bank, is recruiting healthy volunteers to provide life-saving treatment for people with *Clostridioides difficile* infections and other medical conditions. Fecal donors are paid $40 a sample and another $50 bonus if the donor participates five days a week. A OpenBiomme stool donor can make $250 a week or $13,000 a year. Besides healthy stool the typical donor must have regular daily bowel movements and be able to defecate on demand at the OpenBiome facility. Patty Brown, Director or Operations at OpenBiomme noted that women now have an equal opportunity to compete with men to supplement their income using their own natural body products. "Feces have leveled the playing field" she proudly stated.

17. Physician's Privileges Revoked

Ben E. Fitz, MD has been performing surgery for over 45 years. "He was once our best, but he's not the same doctor now," nurse Norma Lee noted. "Recently, we have had scissors and clamps disappear during surgery and our sponge counts are not always correct." Dr. Fitz performed three procedures today and radiographs were obtained after each operation.

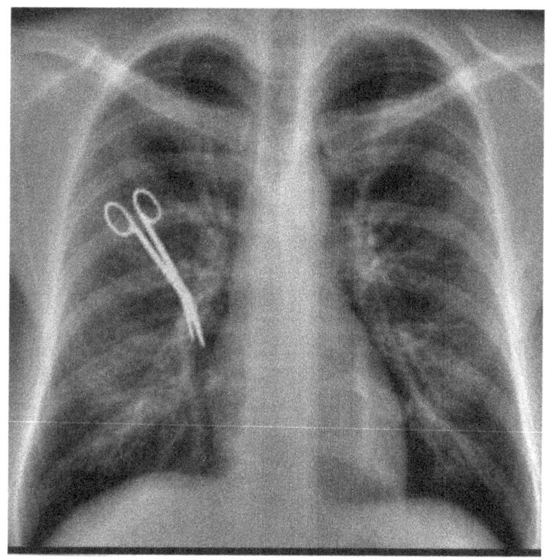

Figure 1. Patient #1 had scissors left in his right chest during a wedge resection of the lung.

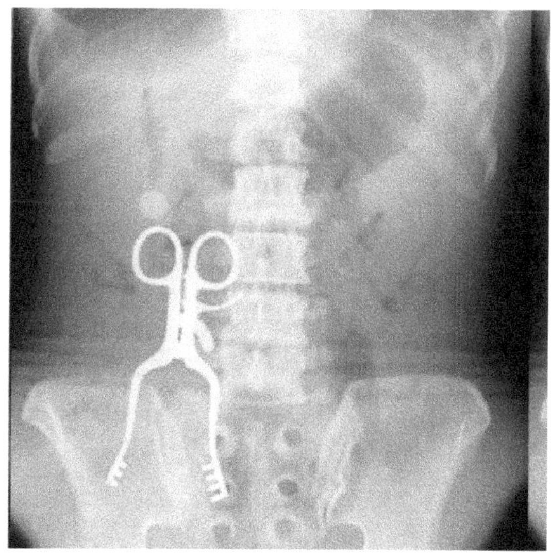

Figure 2. A large retractor is seen in the pelvis following a routine appendectomy in patient #2.

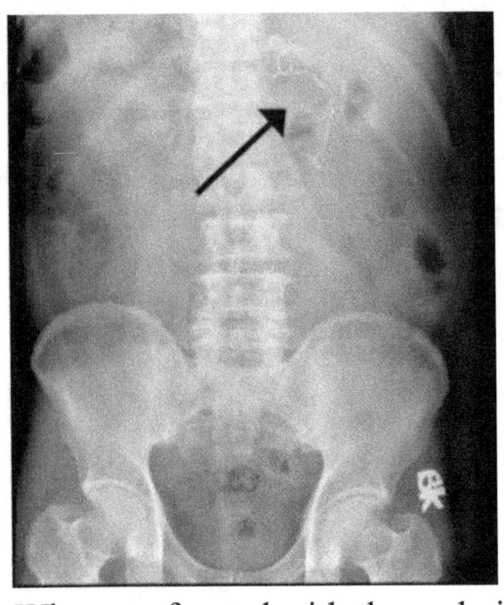

Figure 3. An incorrect sponge count alerted the OR team. The radio-opaque portion of the sponge is noted in the upper abdomen of patient #3.

When confronted with these obvious retained foreign objects an angry Dr. Fitz had a simple explanation. "I'm not surprised. I couldn't concentrate while working. I was distracted by that damn anesthesiologist and all the noise from his monitors that kept alarming." The hospital's Credentials Committee unanimously agreed that a surgeon of Dr. Fitz's reputation and abilities could not have made a surgical error, much less three in one day. The committee placed the blame on "anesthesia". The guilty anesthesiologist was identified and placed on probation. He was ordered to turn off his noisy monitors during surgery. Of course, Dr. Fitz was allowed to continue his practice.

HOSPITAL PRACTICE

18. Major Cause of Operating Room Delay Identified

Alarmed by surgeons' complaints about unnecessary delays in the OR, a blue-ribbon committee of efficiency experts was appointed to study the problem. Despite the fact that none of the members of the panel had ever been inside an OR or had any medical background, the CEO felt their experience in the widget industry would allow them to objectively observe and make recommendations. Their first case was an elective robotic inguinal hernia repair that was scheduled for 90 mins to start at 07:15. The patient was a morbidly obese man with obstructive sleep apnea. He arrived at the hospital at 05:30 and was brought to the pre-operative unit where he was interviewed by the nurse. The attending and resident anesthesiologists came by, started an IV, and discussed the plans and risks of general anesthesia. Everything was ready for an on-time start, except surgical consent and site marking were still needed. Despite numerous calls and pages, the surgical intern did not come to see the patient until 07:20. After he obtained a signed consent and marked the hernia site the team was about to take the patient back when the OR nurse called and told them to delay arrival for another 15 mins because the DaVinci robot still needed to be set-up. Twenty-five minutes later at 07:45 they were given permission to go to the room. Help was needed to transfer the patient from his gurney to the OR table so the "lifting team" was called and they arrived 10 mins later. Once the patient was on the table monitors were applied and an anesthesia time-out was performed. The patient was preoxygenated, anesthetic induction drugs were administered. The anesthesia resident, under the supervision of his attending placed an endotracheal tube on the first attempt, confirmed placement, and secured the airway. The entire process from entering the room to "anesthesia hand-off" took 20 mins. The patient was then re-positioned for the robot, and the scrub nurse began prepping the patient. At 08:25 the attending surgeon arrived and said the patient's position was not acceptable. Re-positioning and re-prepping were completed by 08:35. Following draping and a surgical time-out, surgical incision finally occurred at 08:40. The first-year surgical resident began the repair. This was his first time working with a robot and after 40 mins very little progress had been made. It was now 09:20. The attending surgeon then took over but struggled for almost 40 mins before he decided that the patient's body habitus was too large for a robotic laparoscopic approach. The robot was removed, and an open operation was begun at 10:15. This also proved difficult and the repair was not completed until 11:45. Before the attending surgeon left the OR he assigned the skin closure to a medical student under the supervision of the surgical intern. The medical student, a future psychiatrist, took 30 mins to close the small incisions. It was now 12:15. Once the skin was closed and the drapes removed, the anesthesia team started to wake the patient. Despite his size, his history of sleep apnea, and the length of the procedure the patient emerged from anesthesia and his trachea was extubated in less than 15 mins. The PACU called into the room to inform them that the patient was on "hold" due to lack of PACU nurses. They said they would call back when they were able to accept the patient. That call came 30 mins later at 13:00. Thus, the case scheduled for 90 min took 345 mins. The efficiency observers were shocked. At the postoperative huddle to obtain feedback from the nurses and surgeons, the experts were told that an anesthetic emergence should never have taken so long. The panel concluded that the 15 min wake-up was the major contributors to the prolonged OR time. They recommended that both anesthesiologists undergo 10 hours of mandatory medical re-education focused on teamwork and OR efficiency. The nurses and surgeons were congratulated on their management of this complex patient. Unfortunately, a week later the hernia repair broke down and the surgeon scheduled a re-do robotic surgical repair. Aware of the length of the initial operation he now scheduled the procedure for 120 mins to account for anticipated anesthesia delays.

19. VIP Syndrome

VIP syndrome is the tendency of clinicians to treat influential or famous patients differently because they feel pressured to accede to the VIP's wishes. VIP patients may insist on special privileges and treatment or changes in care plans that can ruin the best-thought-out medical care. Physicians may order too many tests because of anxiety about missing something – or too few tests in order to spare the VIP pain, embarrassment or scrutiny. Recently a famous politician was admitted to our hospital for yet another cosmetic procedure. The Health Insurance Portability and Accountability Act (HIPAA) doesn't allow us to divulge N.P.'s (D-SF) name or medical condition. She insisted on a private suite, and to meet her demands we had to transfer several patients to other facilities to accommodate her and her entourage. Our hospital food was not up to her standards, and an expensive outside catering service was hired to feed her. Despite being an advocate for 'responsible medical care' she insisted on having numerous unnecessary test – and we acquiesced. She complained of severe discomfort and demanded strong opioid analgesics. This led to a drug overdose with a respiratory arrest that required tracheal intubation. The first person to arrive at the code was a medical student who broke several of her teeth during his futile attempts at intubation. Her facial skin was too tight to adequately open her mouth. An endotracheal tube was placed in her esophagus and its position was unrecognized. She experienced several minutes of hypoxemia. Following resuscitation, she was noted to be far less lucid than she had been on admission. Fortunately, her brain damage did not prevent her from returning to work as the majority leader in Congress. The sad part is that this unfortunate set of circumstances could have easily been avoided. For any other patient N.P.'s surgery would have been an outpatient procedure under minor sedation. As a VIP she demanded special attention and suffered the consequences.

20. New Hospital Fiscal Measures

In an institutional-wide effort to balance the budget, hospital CEO Donald Bentwhistle has announced plans to reduce expenditures. First to go, as always, are the non-essential staff. Unfortunately, this measure won't go far enough in solving our money problems and other cutbacks are needed. The operating room is one of the most expensive locations in the hospital and will experience the most drastic changes. The circulating nurse position will be eliminated. Surgeons will now be expected to list all the instruments they might need for a procedure on their preference cards, and requests for additional equipment during surgery will not be honored. The scrub nurse/tech will be replaced by a mid-level poorly paid assistant with a high school or General Educational Development (GED) equivalent since no special skills or training are required just to hand a surgeon his or her tools. Anesthesia will be provided by anyone in the area that is available. "We plan to return to historical practice replacing current inhalation agents with ether, and anyone can administer ether." Finally, purchasing new surgical instruments cannot continue. In orthopedic surgery electric drills and videoscopes will be replaced by less expensive manual instruments. Orthopedic surgeon Dean Carradine reassured Mr. Bentwhistle that he and his colleagues will be able to continue to practice using just basic equipment. Figure.

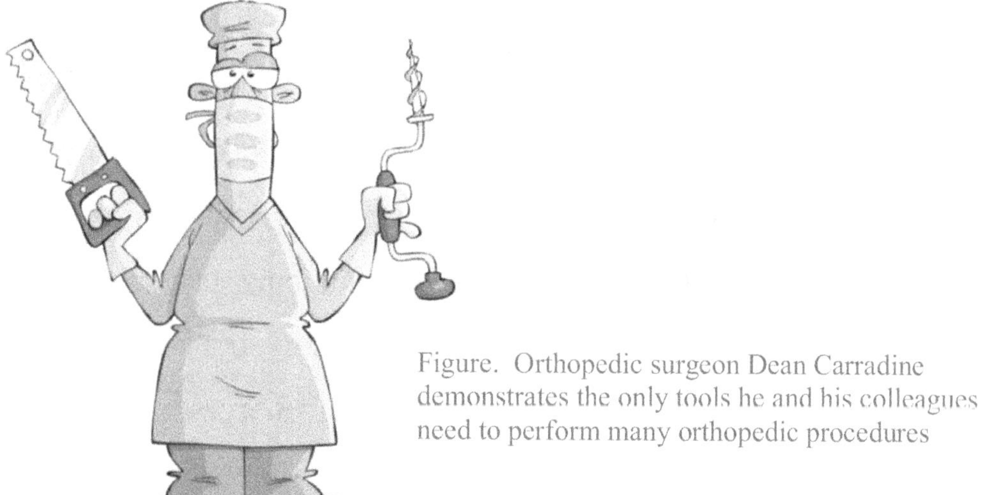

Figure. Orthopedic surgeon Dean Carradine demonstrates the only tools he and his colleagues need to perform many orthopedic procedures

21. Hospital to Offer "Black Friday" Specials

'Black Friday' is the day following Thanksgiving, the busiest shopping day of the year. Stores promote highly anticipated sales and open very early that day. Our elective surgical schedule is markedly reduced since nobody wants an operation when they could be bargain shopping. CEO Donald Bentwhistle brainstormed the problem with his 47 vice-presidents. He said he was open to any suggestions that would fill the ORs. The first recommendation was to bring patients to the hospital by offering discounted cafeteria holiday meals to their families. "Nobody would want to eat our hospital food even if it were free" Bentwhistle observed. Another suggestion was to have the hospital leadership meet and greet visitors while their loved ones underwent surgery. Bentwhistle said the expense of COVID testing every visitor made this fiscally unsound. Plus, he and his administrators preferred not to physically interact with patients and their families. "Potential exposure to coronavirus should be left to our doctors and nurses" he said. Finally, the Vice-President for Perioperative Services said, "Why not offer elective surgery at a discount?" He suggested half-price for uninsured patients, and elimination of any co-pay for those with regular insurance plans. "We make a hell of a lot of money from each operation, so reducing charges to fill our empty ORs will still allow us to turn a profit". Our hospital is near the famous Sanford Shopping Center. A family could drop the patient at the hospital before the stores opened and would still get to the shops early to take advantage of Black Friday sales. "If the sales continue on Saturday, the family can return and shop leisurely all the next day. No overnight inpatient has ever been discharged early in the day anyway." Bentwhistle loved the idea. Advertisements were immediately placed announcing our Black Friday Surgery Sale on selected procedures. The first 20 patients to sign for an operation will also receive an additional 20% discount on all medical charges.

22. Robots to Replace Healthcare Workers

Direct interaction with COVID+ patients is one of the riskiest parts of a healthcare worker's job. Recently, robots have been used to remotely monitor and care for potentially infected patients, removing physicians and nurses from the risk of exposure. The economic advantages of extending robotic care to all patients, not just COVID+ patients, was immediately recognized by hospital leadership. In California a hospital-based registered nurse earns a base salary between $75,000-100,000 per year, with the potential for making more by taking night and weekend call or by working overtime. Physician salaries are significantly higher. C.F.O. Rob R. Baron observed, "For the cost of a single robot, a mere $1-2 million dollars, we can replace dozens of nurses and doctors. Each robot will pay for itself in less than a year." Robots can monitor vital signs, do virtual physical exams, dispense medications, deliver food, clean and bathe the patient, and even provide bedside companionship for demented patients with fall precautions. The option of adding Siri with an extensive medical database enables the robot to intelligently answer the patients' questions. "The robot can provide better responses than a medical student, or a sleep deprived intern, or even an uninterested resident could." A local company has developed a clinical nursing robot they named the Nightingale®. Figure 1. A more advanced robot capable of independent surgery, the Cushing®, will soon be ready. Figure 2. The anesthesia robot, the Einstein® is still in development but will require more time to complete the very large information database needed for safe anesthesia. "Our goal is to replace all human healthcare providers by 2025." Baron continued, "Profits from eliminating expensive, but no longer needed nurses and physicians will allow us to recruit and fill our projected needs for more administrative staff and will enable us to give our present leadership additional salary bonuses they deserve for their work on this project."

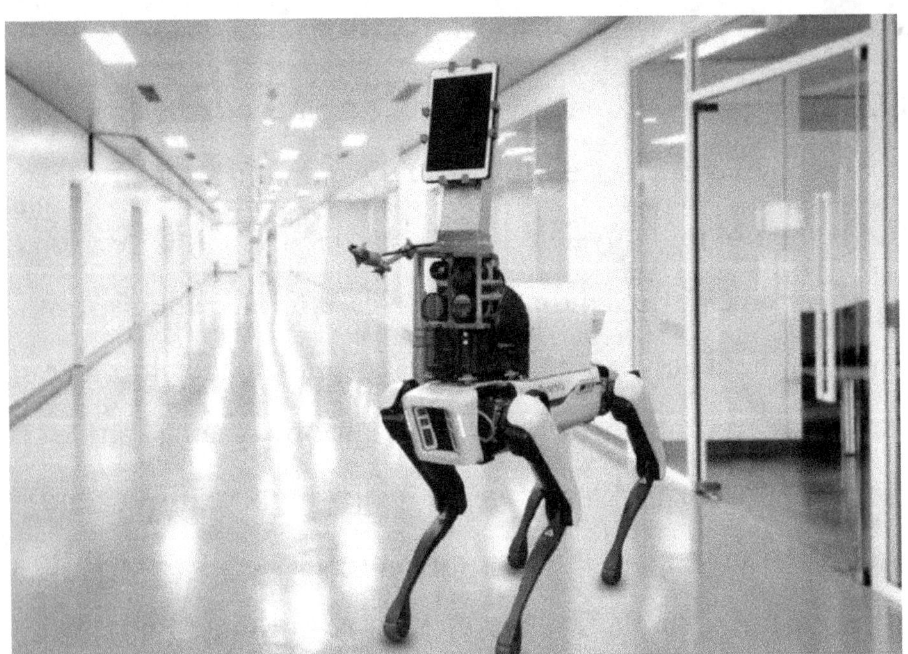

Figure 1. The nursing robot, the Nightingale®, can replace expensive healthcare workers.

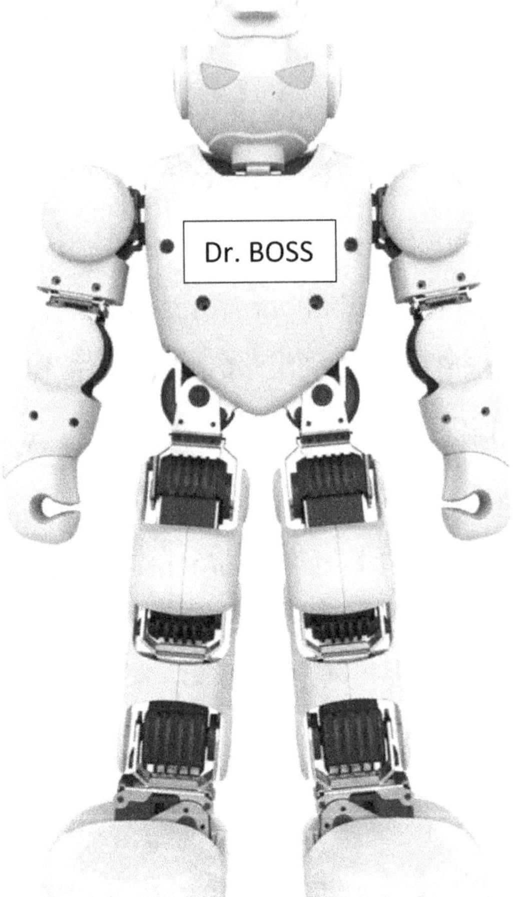

Figure 2. The surgical robot, the Cushing® is shown accompanied by his physician assistant robot, Sally P.A.®.

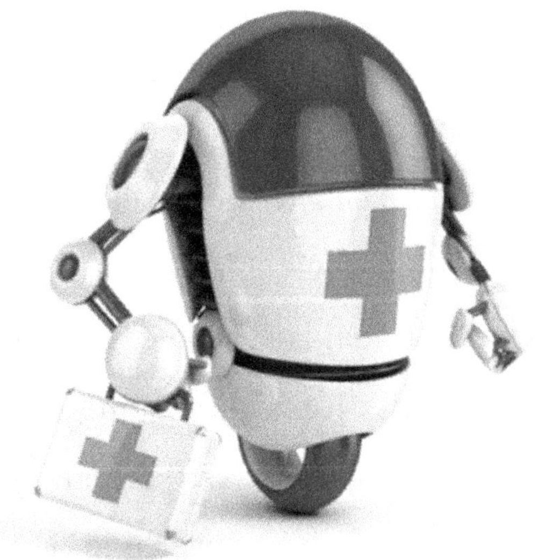

ORTHOPEDIC SURGERY

23. Orthopedic Surgeons Fight COVID

The American Society of Surgeons (A.S.S.) held their annual meeting last week in Portland, Oregon during the height of the current COVID crisis. CDC recommendations to wear face coverings, to social distance, and to avoid large public meetings were basically being ignored by many of the otherwise peaceful citizens in that city. To show support for these government guidelines the orthopedic section of A.S.S. voted to help enforce COVID guidelines. They organized a 'Committee on Guideline Enforcement', armed themselves, and immediately took to the streets of Portland to ensure that everyone wore facial coverings. Figure. These brave orthopods attempted to break up any large groups they encountered. The Federal government as well as their surgical colleagues at A.S.S. expressed appreciation to these dedicated young physicians for taking on the battle to combat COVID. These men left the safety and security of their hospitals, clinics, and gyms, to work the mean streets of Portland.

Figure. Orthopedic surgery residents patrol the streets of Portland to enforce the face-mask mandate.

24. Orthopedic or Neurosurgeon for Back Pain?

My friends and family often ask me for health care advice. A common question is, "Should I see an orthopedic surgeon or a neurosurgeon for my back pain?" It's a difficult question to answer. Both these specialties treat and operate on patients with back pain and often compete with each other for the same patients. There are some key differences between these two surgical specialties that a patient should know before making a choice. An orthopedic surgical residency is shorter, usually 5 years while a neurosurgical residency is 6-8 years depending on the program. Both need to complete an additional year of Fellowship in order to specialize in back surgery. Orthopedic surgeons usually have had a college education. At college they played competitive sports before entering medical school. In contrast, neurosurgeons spent their college years in libraries and taking additional academic courses. Following entry into an orthopedic residency program the young surgeon must attend gymnasium at least 3 times a week for strength training, while a neurosurgeon spends that time doing research. The successful neurosurgeon does make more money than the average orthopedic surgeon but has less free time to enjoy the fruits of his or her labor. The orthopedic surgeon spends almost all of his clinical time performing surgery and depends on his physician assistant and a hospitalist to treat his patients' medical problems. Orthopedic surgeons are often referred to as "bone docs" while a neurosurgeon is called a "brain surgeon". Those appellations describe the differences their colleagues see in their intellectual capabilities. To return to the original question, "orthopedic surgeon or neurosurgeon?" it boils down to a choice between brains and brawn. As for my advice, when a friend or family member asks me who I would recommend I usually say, "avoid any unnecessary surgery and go to a chiropractor."

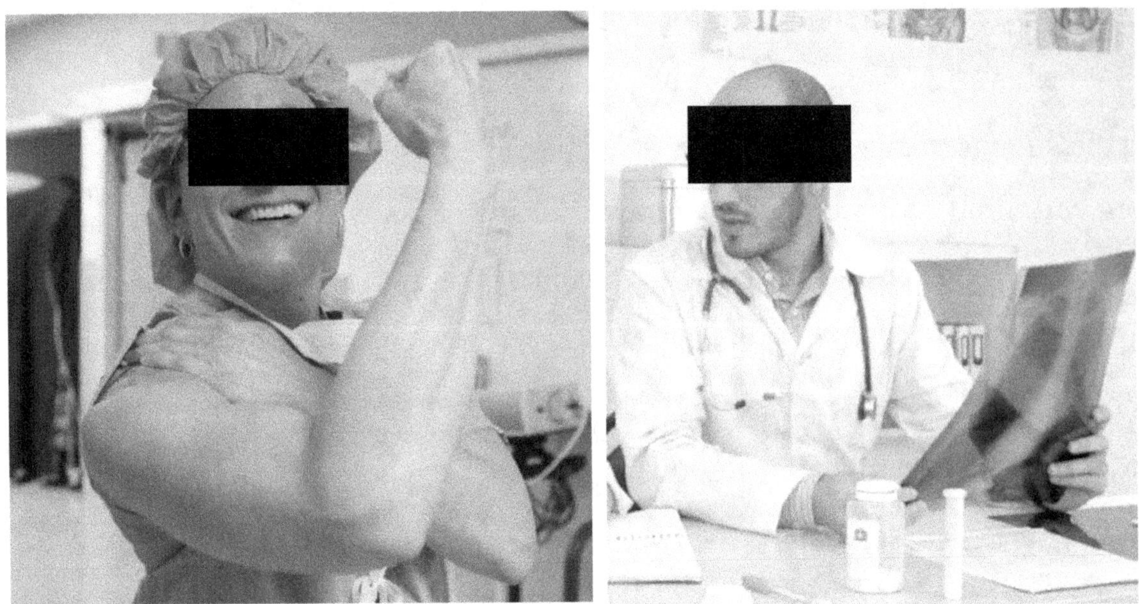

Figure. In the operating room orthopedic surgeon Dean Carradine flexes his biceps celebrating the successful completion of a challenging case (left), while in the adjacent room neurosurgeon Gary Sternberg reviews his patient's postoperative x'ray films to check and confirm his repair (right).

25. Surgeons Evolved to be Taller

Human evolution is apparently progressing at an exponential rate. Although modern surgical practice is no more than 150 years old, a study found important changes in the members of the surgical health care team that they attributed to evolution. A published study from Spain found that surgeons tend to be taller and more attractive than other physicians (1). The researchers hypothesized that being taller and better-looking gave surgeons an *'evolutionary advantage'*, in that "they will have better views of the patient on the operating room table and the rest of the OR, as well as making them more distinguishable and 'respected' as the leader in the room." The report went further in describing how evolution has been at work sculpting the entire operating room team. It found that OR nurses were not as attractive as nurses working in other health care areas. The researchers believe that this has an evolutionary advantage since less attractive female nurses are less likely to distract the handsome surgeon from concentrating on his operation. In support of this theory, they also found that although male surgeons often marry nurses, those nurses usually worked outside the OR on hospital wards and in clinics. Not surprisingly, anesthesiologists have evolved to be more intelligent than surgeons. This is an obvious advantage since patients' lives depend on the anesthesiologist. "You wouldn't expect the most important person in the OR to be the least intelligent" the study's author noted. Data shows the greatest statistical difference in IQ is between anesthesiologists and orthopedic surgeons. The latter, although being better looking and taller, had the lowest IQ of anyone on the health care team. "You don't need to use your brain if you are an orthopedic surgeon," the study's authors argued, "so evolution is truly is at work in the OR".

1. Trilla A, et al. Phenotypic Differences between Male Physicians, Surgeons, and Film Stars: Comparative Study. BMJ (2006) 333: 1291-3. doi: 10.1136/bmj.39015.672373.80

26. Orthopedic Surgeon to Continue Family Legacy

In 1945 orthopedic surgeon Dr. Adolf Schicklgruber was awarded the prestigious 'Josef Mengele Prize' for surgery. Unlike digitally handicapped surgeons, the ambidextrous Schicklgruber had 6 fingers on each hand. Each hand could handle a scalpel or drill while simultaneously holding a retractor. Figure 1. Schicklgruber could perform the most complex orthopedic procedures without any assistance. At that time Schicklgruber's wife Klara was pregnant with their first child, and everyone was anxious to see if their offspring would also be blessed with functional polydactyly. They were! A spokesman for the Mengele Foundation for Medical Excellence, based in Brazil, said "Our goal is to produce genetically superior individuals. If we can selectively raise orthopedic surgeons able to complete operations single-handedly, we will conquer the world … of medicine!" All 6 of

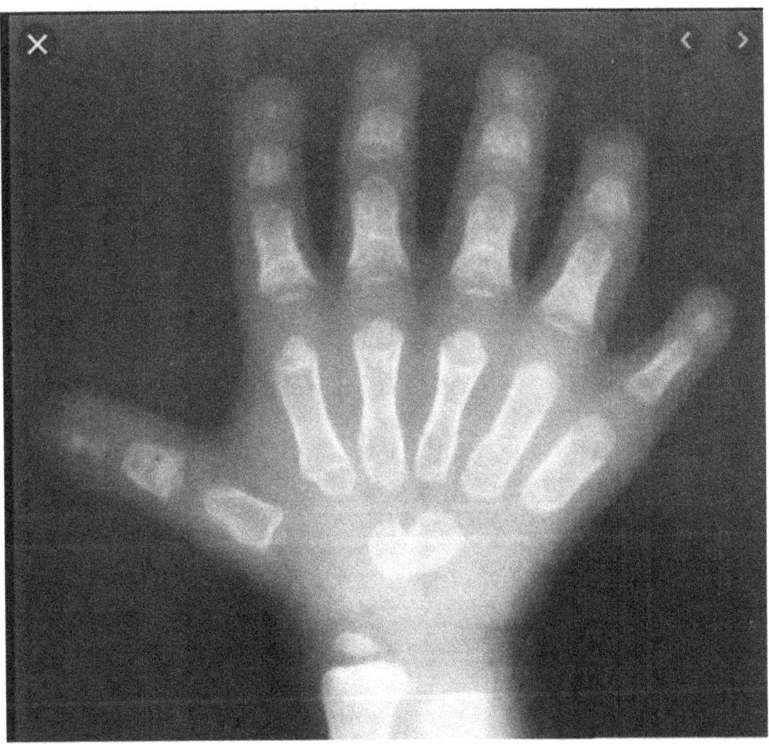

the children subsequently born to the Schicklgruber's had extra digits. The Mengele Foundation genetically interbred Schicklgrubers, and today the Foundation proudly announced the entry of Dr. Adolph Schicklgruber, IV, into Sao Paulo's German Hospital's orthopedic

Figure 1. The award-winning orthopedic surgeon Adolph Schicklgruber was blessed with ambidextrous polydactyly. His descendants all had multiple digits.

residency program. The spokesman said, "He is the product of over seven decades of experimentation. We have confidence that the latest Doktor Schicklgruber will continue the family tradition of orthopedic surgical excellence. The Foundation shared the following photos as evidence that their efforts have been successful. Figure 2.

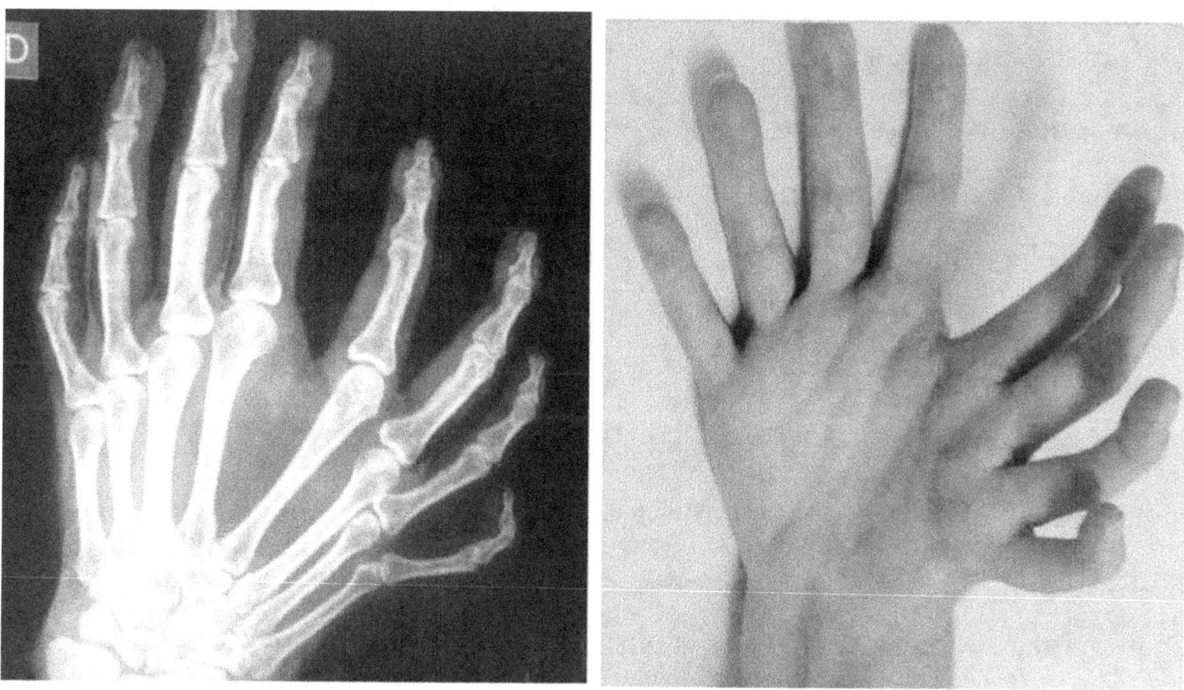

Figure 2. After several generations of successful interbreeding, future orthopedic surgeon Doktor Adolph Schicklgruber IV has eight functional fingers on each hand.

27. Surgeon Forced to Change Specialty

Surgeons, anesthesiologists, and nurses wear face masks working in the operating room. Now, the COVID crisis has forced everyone including those same healthcare professionals to wear masks in public. Carbon dioxide can accumulate under the masks and breathing excessive amounts of carbon dioxide can reduce the amount of oxygen inhaled. Reduced oxygen levels ("hypoxia") can have a deleterious effect on brain function. For some people even mild hypoxia can have serious consequences. One of our general surgeons, "Doctor X" recently experienced "mask induced hypoxia syndrome" (M.I.H.S.). After wearing a mask in the OR, he now had to wear a mask on the wards and in clinics while seeing patients. Then, after leaving the hospital he had to wear another mask. Dr. X suffered cognitive and physical impairment. He was no longer able to perform delicate operations. He could not focus on his patients' complaints, form a differential diagnosis, or create a treatment plan. Even basic verbal communication with his co-workers became difficult. With a shortage of physicians during the COVID crisis the Committee on Physician Well-Being pondered over how an obviously incapacitated Dr. X could still contribute. They decided to allow Dr. X to continue operating, but now working as an orthopedic surgeon. Their report stated that "fixing bones is not delicate surgery. An orthopod doesn't ever need to make a diagnosis – that's what a radiologist is for. Orthopods don't treat any medical problems – hospitalists do that for them. Since orthopedic surgeons never talk to their OR team there will be no problem with lack of communication either." The committee has created a fast-track training program to direct physically and mentally impaired healthcare workers into orthopedic surgery. Anyone suffering from M.I.H.S. can continue in orthopedics until they can demonstrate a return of normal brain function. For many like Dr. X this will not happen until the requirements to wear face masks at all times are rescinded.

PROGRESSIVISM

28. Hospital Initiates Anti-Microaggression Policy

'Microaggression' is a term used for brief and commonplace daily verbal or behavioral indignities, whether intentional or unintentional, that communicate hostile, derogatory, or negative attitudes toward a member of a stigmatized or culturally marginalized group. They are difficult to detect by members of the dominant culture, who are often unaware they are causing harm. No group faces more hospital microaggressions than surgical interns. The slightest error on their part often results in a negative comment or even criticism by their attending surgeon, a truly dominant figure. Although surgeons believe that constructive criticism is an important part of the education of future surgeons, sensitive interns can be upset or even hurt by these actions. A case in point. Yesterday, intern Bruce Gentile accidently gave his patient ten times the normal dose of a beta blocker. The patient became markedly hypotensive and had a stroke. Gentile's attending surgeon asked him to be more careful in the future when prescribing potent medications. Gentile was quite upset, not because he nearly killed the patient, but because the attending blamed him for a mistake that he felt anyone could have made. "He should have been more understanding," Gentile complained. Later that day, in surgery, Gentile was not paying attention and inadvertently cut a major artery. This resulted in massive blood loss requiring life-saving resuscitative measures. His attending suggested that Gentile pay more attention when assisting in surgery. Then in the recovery room another patient suffered a respiratory arrest. Gentile was first to arrive on the scene. He attempted to intubate the patient's trachea but placed the endotracheal tube in the esophagus. When the respiratory therapist said she couldn't ventilate the patient, Gentile insisted he had put the tube in the correct position. He said the problem with ventilation was with the therapist. The patient remained hypoxic until an anesthesiologist arrived and successfully replaced the tube. The attending physician informed Gentile that he should have listened to the experienced respiratory therapist. All these aggressions were too much for Gentile. He complained to the hospital's Microaggression Committee that he was the target of a dominant attending surgeon's cruel and hateful attacks. He believed as a surgical intern he was a member of an under-represented minority group. "We have no rights" Gentile complained. The committee agreed that the attending surgeon's behavior was clearly inappropriate. To combat these practices, the hospital has instituted new guidelines. Now, under no circumstances can a house officer be criticized for their actions, no matter how blatant or harmful they are. Rather, the micro-aggressive attending surgeon was ordered to apologize to Gentile. The committee said Gentile's lack of attention and hubris were all 'normal' human behaviors, and as such, were completely acceptable.

29. Hospitals Add Disclaimers

Companies and brands like Aunt Jemima and Uncle Ben's Rice have recently distanced themselves from racist stereotypes by changing their branding. Disney Corporation in its ongoing commitment to diversity and inclusion announced that it is adding a disclaimer to some of its old movies that include racist stereotypes. Movies like "Aristocats" which features racist caricatures of East Asian people, "Dumbo," in which crows perform a musical number in the style of a racist minstrel show, and "Peter Pan" for its stereotypical portrayal of Native peoples were included. Similarly, the American Medical Association has apologized for the many wrongs that racist American physicians have been guilty of in the past. They cited Walter Reed Medical Center, named after Major Walter Reed, a U.S. Army physician who in 1901 confirmed the theory of a Cuban doctor, Carlos Finlay, that yellow fever is transmitted by a mosquito. The hospital will henceforth be known as 'Carlos Finlay Centro Medico' to honor the contributions of that under-represented Hispanic medical pioneer. Rush Medical College was named for Benjamin Rush, MD, the only physician to sign the Declaration of Independence. Rush was a social reformer, humanitarian, and educator. He spoke out against the slave trade and was a member of the Pennsylvania Abolition Society. All that now doesn't matter since he is guilty by his association with other Declaration signers who were wealthy, and White, and slave-owning, and men! Patients admitted to the Rush Medical Center will now be greeted at the hospital entrance with a sign disavowing any hospital support for the Declaration of Independence. 'Indigenous Peoples Hospital', previously known as Columbia University Hospital, will require that all its employees complete a medical education course entitled 'Christopher Columbus, Colonizer and Mass Murderer'. A hospital spokesman said, "while it can't change the past, we can acknowledge it, learn from it, and move forward together."

30. Hospital Changes Logo

Figure 1. The former Washington Hospital logo honored local Native American residents.

Washington Hospital in Broken Arrow, South Dakota was one of the first health care institutions built on tribal land dedicated to the care of reservation occupants. The local people were proud of the Washington Hospital logo and nickname, which seemed appropriate for this landmark facility. Figure 1. That all changed recently. Interest in social justice has led many communities and organizations to rename schools, military bases, parks, and even hospitals when the original name is considered offensive. A vocal group of Washington Hospital physicians and nurses have questioned the appropriateness of their hospital's nickname the Washington Hospital 'Redskins'. It is insulting and hurtful. They pointed out that that most of the health care professionals working at the hospital are not and have never been Native People (formally known as Indians).

The group argued that the hospital's nickname and logo should be representative of its minority staff members. Reluctantly, hospital administration bowed to their demands and a sweatshirt with the new hospital logo was just introduced. Figure 2.

Figure 2. The new Washington Hospital Logo features a likeness of Dr. Bradford Smith IV, chief of surgery.

31. New Recommendations to Avoid Offensive Disease Names

An *eponymous disease* is a medical disorder, condition, or syndrome, named after the physician(s) who first identified the disease, or a patient who suffered from the disease, a fictional character who exhibited signs of the disease, a location associated with the condition, or even an actor portraying someone with the disease. Despite the current world-wide COVID crisis, the World Health Organization (WHO) is directing a major effort at eliminating the insult and stigma inflicted by diseases named for people, places, and animals. WHO demands that researchers, health officials, and journalists use neutral, generic, *'non-hurtful'* terms (1). Some recommendations to change long established eponymous conditions are reasonable. 'Wegener's granulomatosis' is named after **Dr Friedrich Wegener** a Nazi sympathizer, and Hans Reiter ('Reiter's Syndrome') was a Nazi party leader and convicted war criminal. But WHO's goal of total political correctness can be taken to extremes. For example, WHO believes 'swine flu' gives pigs a bad reputation. "The so-called swine flu is not transmitted by pigs, yet some countries still ban pork imports or slaughtered pigs after the 2009 outbreak; and the Jews and Muslims still to this day refuse to eat pork" a WHO representative complained. He continued by describing how 'monkey pox' demeans our closest animal relatives, and how 'Rift Valley Fever' has negatively impacted the tourism industry in Somalia. Many Arab countries are unhappy about 'Middle East Respiratory Syndrome' and have cited M.E.R.S. as the major impediment to finding lasting peace in the region. Recently we have seen how the 'China Virus' has stigmatized millions of innocent Chinese who had nothing to do with their leaders introducing the novel coronavirus to the world. The WHO guidelines state that any name of any disease, new or old, must never offend anyone. For example, 'Pickwickian syndrome', is named after a fictional literary figure. It stigmatizes morbidly obese patients with 'obesity hypoventilation syndrome' who have no idea who Charles Dickens was. The WHO believes it is unfair to honor a single physician when others were involved in describing the disorder. WHO points out that 'Behçet's disease', an inflammation of the blood vessels, should more accurately be known as "Hippocrates-Janin-Neumann-Reis-Bluthe-Gilbert-Planner-Remenovsky-Weve-Shigeta-Pils-Grütz-Carol-Ruys-Samek-Fischer-Walter-Roman-Kumer-Adamantiades-Dascalopoulos-Matras-Whitwell-Nishimura-Blobner-Weekers-Reginster-Knapp-Behçet's disease" to account for all the researchers who contributed to the understanding of that medical condition. The WHO then went on to apologize to anyone whose name was unintentionally omitted from the new name of the condition previously known as 'Behçet's Disease'.

1. Krisberg K. Scientists need to rethink how human disease names chosen, WHO advises: New best practice. **The Nation's Health August (2015) 45 (6) 1-16**

32. Referring to Famous Composers by Last Name is 'White Supremacy'

A music theory professor argued in a recent article that referring to famous composers by only their last names is a form of White supremacy that needs to be remedied. The (inappropriately named) Chris *White*, who teachers at the University of Massachusetts Amherst, suggested that well-known composers like Bach, Mozart, and Beethoven, ought to be referred to by their full names to put them on an equal footing with lesser-known composers. "White male composers are introduced with only surnames," while "everyone else" – i.e., "women and composers of color" – are referred to by their full name." Such two-tiered nomenclature, White (I'm sorry, I should call him Mr. Chris (White)) argued, is indicative of "centuries of systematic prejudice, exclusion, sexism, and racism" within music. Mr. Chris neglected to mention that many Black musicians and entertainers are known only by their first names – thereby placing them on an unequal footing than lesser-known White musicians. Examples include Beyonce, Rhianna, Prince, Sade, Usher just to name a few. To avoid claims of racism in medicine, the American Medical Association has requested the immediate use of the full name of all diseases known only by a surname. The list is quite long, but examples include the following. Hansen's Disease (formerly known as leprosy) will be referred to as 'Gerhard Armauer Hansen's Disease', Crohn's Disease as **'Burrill Bernard Crohn's Disease', and** François Gigot de la Peyronie's full name will replace 'Peyronie's Disease'. Since each of these physicians were White men, calling the diseases they discovered or significantly contributed to by only their last name would be racist according to Mr. Chris (White).

33. Medical Schools to Eliminate Grading

Many schools are changing their names in attempts to be 'anti-racist'. The San Diego Unified School District is going one giant step further by re-examining routine educational practices. Under their new system students *will not* be penalized for failing to complete assignments, and teachers will give them extra opportunities to demonstrate *'mastery'* of subjects. Grading will no longer consider average test and assignment scores. Instead, letter grades will reflect a student's *mastery* of the subject rather than their completion of homework, quizzes, or tests. What constitutes *mastery* is left unexplained. Grades "shall not be influenced by behavior or factors that directly measure students' knowledge and skills in the content area." Leniency will be given to students who don't do the course work, including those who don't even show up at all to school since attendance is no longer a factor in grading. These progressive societal steps have been hailed by influential educational groups like 'Medical Education for Special Students' (M.E.S.S.). Historically medical students have been required to learn anatomy, physiology, pathology, pharmacology … the list is endless. Future physicians had to become familiar with the diagnosis and treatment of scores of conditions. They had to plan a logical course of action in dealing with a patient's problems and be able to communicate their management plans to other healthcare workers. Medical education makes more demands on a student in training than in almost any other field. This is obviously unfair to disadvantaged medical students. M.E.S.S. recommends elimination of all testing or any other measure of competency, since they believe conventional medical education (like conventional mathematics) is a racist construct. When a student feels he or she is ready to practice medicine they should be immediately licensed. A student should begin practice of a specialty (surgery, anesthesia, radiology, etc) as soon as they graduate, whether or not they have mastered that field. Actually,

M.E.S.S. correctly disagrees with the San Diego school system since '*mastery*' is a racist term with slavery connotations, and as such, '*lack of mastery*' must not interfere with a medical career. And of course, the traditional 'White Coat' ceremony when a newly minted medical school graduate receives a white laboratory coat to mark the transition from the study of preclinical to clinical health sciences is now strictly taboo. Figure. Although the white coat symbolizes the purity of purpose being affirmed by becoming a health professional, this ceremony is obviously racist and will be replaced with the grey hoodie or black niqab ceremony.

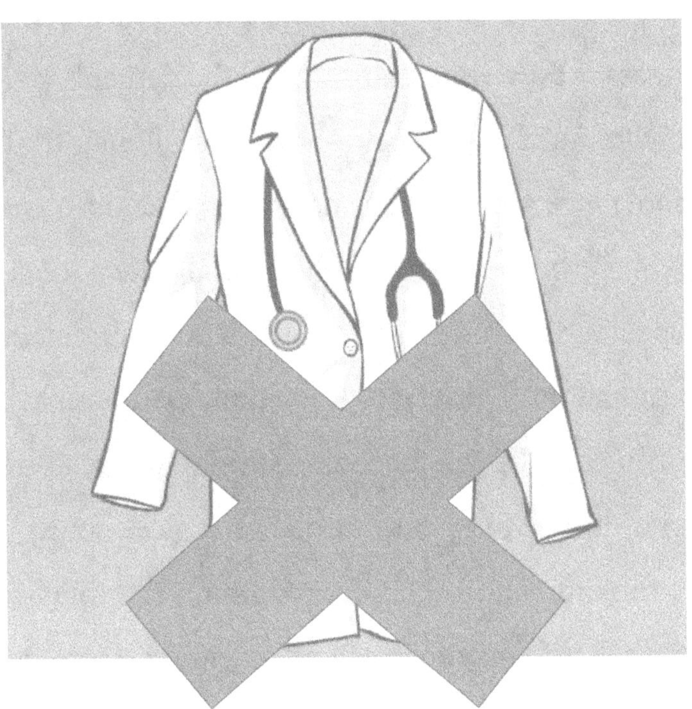

34. Brothers Pose for Family Portrait

It was a nostalgic reunion at the Simian household as twin brothers Harry and Jimmy (aka 'Baldy') posed for a photograph. Figure 1. Harry has been majoring in *Cultural Studies* at UC Berkeley, a prestigious university in the San Francisco Bay area. He chose Cultural Studies, an interdisciplinary field that investigates the ways in which culture creates and transforms individual experiences, everyday life, social relations and power, because of brother Baldy's serious medical problem. Since childhood Baldy has suffered from alopecia, the loss of hair due to stress. This condition has affected his social and employment opportunities, and he continues to experience humiliation and loss of self-esteem. Harry has vowed to "level the playing field" and "right the wrong". Baldy is undergoing psychotherapy and now realizes that lack of hair in no way makes him different than the rest of his family and society. Jimmy plans to continue his education with a scholarship for under-

Figure 1. Brothers Harry and Jimmy Simian pose for family portrait. Jimmy (aka "Baldy") plans to join his brother in the U.C. Berkeley Cultural Studies program.

represented minorities with medical disabilities (in his case alopecia), joining Harry at Berkeley. Harry has assured Baldy that he will "fit *right* in" on campus. (Ed Note: nothing is 'right' at Berkeley) The chair of the school's Diversity Committee, Professor William White (below) was excited to learn of Harry's decision to attend Berkeley. Figure 2.

Figure 2. Professor White, who suffers from albinism, says he knows what it is like not to be accepted at Berkeley because of your appearance. He is shown welcoming Harry on his first day of class.

35. Syndromes Cloud Disney's Legacy

Walt Disney was an American entrepreneur, animator, writer, voice actor, and film producer. During his lifetime he was beloved and respected for his many contributions. It is true that Disney was accused of racism because some of his early productions contained racially insensitive material. For example, 'Song of the South' was criticized for its perpetuation of black stereotypes. But those were unintentional mistakes and have been forgiven. What cannot be forgiven or forgotten is the role Disney played in destroying the psychological health of generations of the world's children through the characters in his films. The group 'Concerned and Responsible Adult Zealots for Youngsters' (C.R.A.Z.Y) has listed some of the many destructive syndromes Disney popularized.

- **Peter Pan Syndrome**: Peter Pan is a boy who wouldn't grow up. The syndrome is characterized by emotional immaturity and an unwillingness to take on responsibilities.

- **Wendy Syndrome**: Women who act like mothers to their partners and others.

- **Sleeping Beauty Syndrome**: Sleeping Beauty pricks her finger and falls into a deep sleep, only to be woken by a prince's kiss years later. This syndrome is characterized by periods of excessive sleep and altered behavior. The patient sleeps for most of the day and night and will only wake up to eat or go to the bathroom. Episodes can last up to months at a time, inhibiting the ability to work or go to school.

- **Rapunzel Syndrome**: This is a condition that results from people eating hair ('trichophagia'). The hair accumulates resulting in a giant hair ball in the stomach or small intestine (trichobezoar), which must be removed surgically.

- **Bambi Complex**: Bambi is a cute little deer whose mother is shot and killed. People with 'Bambi Complex' are very sentimental and sympathetic towards wild animals. They usually have very strong feelings against hunting, controlled fires, and any perceived inhumane treatment of animals.

- **Cinderella Complex**: A person with Cinderella Complex is very dependent on men for emotional and financial purposes. It is also associated with the desire to be swept away and saved by a Prince Charming.

C.R.A.Z.Y. and many other organizations claiming to represent the public have demanded that all classic Disney films and cartoons be immediately withdrawn from circulation. They believe that the world's children will be healthier without Snow White (Ed note: snow is WHITE and so it must be racist), or Prince Charming (Ed note: he is a male gender fascist), or Tinker Bell (Ed note: demeans Gay men). The need to remove all the Seven Dwarfs is obvious. Walt Disney's name must also be removed from all locations. They suggested renaming his parks with non-threatening, socially acceptable names like "You-Can-Be-Anyone-You-Want-to-Be-Land" for Disneyland, and "End-Global-Warming-World" for Disneyworld. A well-known supporter for these changes is Swedish teenager Greta Thunberg who proudly announced that none of her numerous psychologic problems can be attributed to a Disney film. It seems she has never been to a movie or visited an amusement park.

ANIMAL RIGHTS

36. Therapy Dogs for Bariatric Patients

Following the initial success of our hospital's 'therapy dog' initiative, we have expanded the program to include visits to all surgical wards. Hospitalized patients cannot to bring their own pets to visit during their recovery from surgery, so in order to make our bariatric patients feel comfortable we have recruited a team of special dogs. In addition to the usual requirements that they be well-trained, obedient and gentle, bariatric therapy dogs must also physically resemble bariatric patients. Patients bond with these animals since both can experience similar physical and emotional challenges related to their condition. Pictured below are 'Brutus' and 'Fang', two of our most popular bariatric therapy dogs. Both are resting following a strenuous 2 minutes of exercise with patients recovering from gastric bypass surgery. Figure.

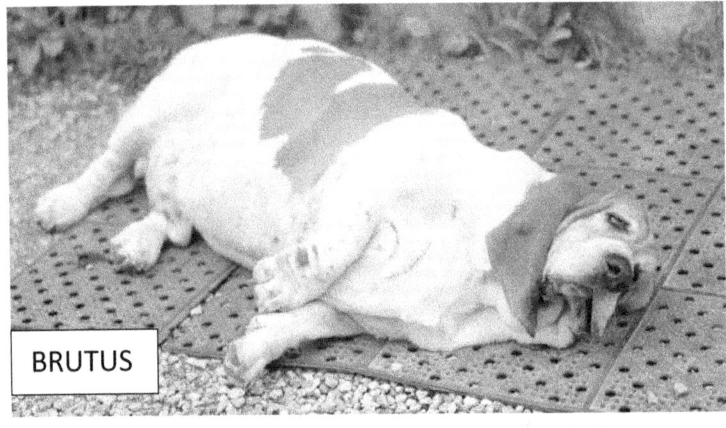

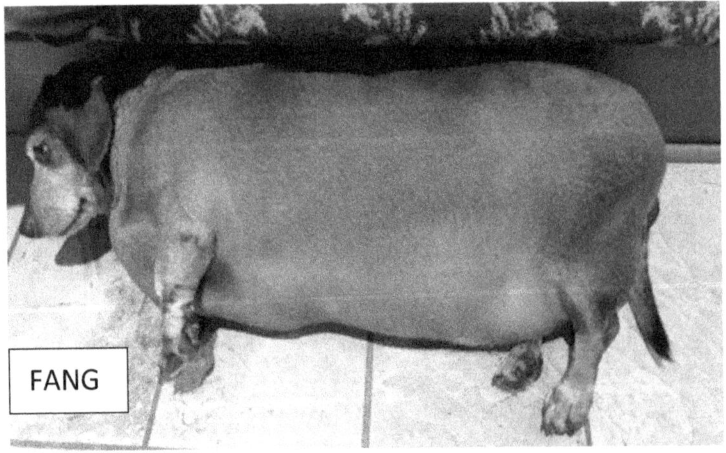

Figure. Brutus and Fang, two of the most popular bariatric therapy dogs rest after strenuous activity

Costco pulling products allegedly made with forced monkey labor

37. Costco Pulling Products Made with Forced Monkey Labor

The use of 'forced monkey labor' has led Costco to stop selling Thai-made coconut products. People for the Ethical Treatment of Animals -Monkey and Apes Division (PETA-MAD) has been tracking animal abuse in Thailand and it now urges retailers to pull merchandise to discourage the practice. "No consumer wants monkeys to be chained up and treated like coconut-picking machines," spokesperson Greta Barnyard said in a statement. PETA-MAD's investigation found that chained monkeys can pick as many as 400 coconuts a day. After their 16-hour shift, they are stuffed into cages until their next shift. "Just because something is legal or accepted doesn't mean it's OK," said Kent Swine, PETA-MAD's corporate responsibility officer. Encouraged by the success of their sister organization, People for the Ethical Treatment of Interns: Medical Division (PETI-MD) has initiated a similar project to stop abuse of hospital interns. "If we can stop people from taking advantage of trained monkeys, then we certainly should treat our trained interns as decently." These poor men and women see up to 50 patients a day, and then are locked in cramped, smelly call-rooms until their next shift. "Patients should avoid hospitals practicing 'forced intern labor' – it's just not right!" PETI-MD recommends patronizing those few hospitals where interns and residents are treated humanely. A proposition is on this year's ballot, if passed, insures that house officers, like monkeys, work only 16-hour shifts and then have 8 hours off to sleep until their next workday. Proponents demand that house officers be fed, clothed, and treated with dignity. After all, "our house officers are not monkeys!" When the American

Monkey Association (Ed note: the lesser known A.M.A.) heard about the comparison between monkeys and interns they were aghast. "Monkeys have it much better than interns for a reason. They work hard and are rewarded with their favorite food. Unlike hospital interns, monkeys don't work for peanuts". In response our hospital cafeterias began serving free bananas to all house staff. Figure.

Figure. The hospital's cafeteria now offers free bananas to all house staff

38. Denmark to Cull Minks as a Coronavirus Safety Measure

[News: Nov. 6, 2020] The mink industry is important to the economy of Denmark, the largest producer of mink skins in the world.   The public was shocked by Denmark's announcement that it plans to kill millions of minks due to fears that a mutated coronavirus strain in these animals may pose a potential danger to humans. "All Danish minks will be culled, including non-infected and otherwise healthy animals," Denmark's Foreign Minister Jaspar Fuur said at a press conference. "We would rather go a step too far than take a step too little to combat COVID-19." He added that his progressive, enlightened Scandinavian country had not overreacted nor taken the decision lightly even though the World Health Organization (WHO) questioned the move. Tyra Kraut, a senior public health specialist at Denmark's State Serum Institute, the authority that identified the mutated strain, said more research was needed. "This is a global pandemic and many millions of different animals have been exposed," stated Dr. Mike Rumour, executive director of the WHO Health Emergencies Program. "Right now, the evidence that we have doesn't suggest that this mink variant is in any way different in the way it behaves ... it is still the same virus." WHO added that the coronavirus risk from other farm animals and livestock was generally low, but mutations in all animals are normally always present. Alarmed after hearing the news that COVID mutations can occur in other farm animals, proactive Norway immediately announced its decision to kill all chickens, ducks and geese in their country. "We know different coronaviruses are present in poultry, so the potential for another mutation is too great for us to take a chance." Not to be outdone by their neighbors, Sweden announced its plans to destroy every animal in their country. "We have already culled our bats, pangolins, and swine, because of coronavirus, but those interventions were just the beginning. Next, we will destroy all wild and domesticated animals," Swedish spokes-them Ole Dumson said. Representatives from People for the Ethical Treatment of Animals (PETA) applauded this decision but stated that they were too long in coming. "Now is the time for the leaders of all countries to take similar steps." Politicians in these cold northern Scandinavian countries then realized that these actions would eliminate the entire supply of mink pelts. They then demanded that minks, and only minks, be exempted from the animal culling in order that their fur be available for their wives and girlfriends winter coats.

Figure. Minks at a farm in Denmark react with fear and disbelief after being informed that he would soon be "eliminated" to stem a coronavirus mutation

39. Salk's Statue Destroyed

The toppling of statues of famous historic figures who are now considered by some to have been evil or oppressors reached a new level of insanity yesterday when the statue of Jonas Salk, the physician who cured polio, was destroyed. Figure. The radical group 'People for the Ethical Treatment of Laboratory Animals' (PETLA) took responsibility for this act. Their reason is that before Salk perfected and released his life-saving polio vaccine to the public, he tested it on laboratory animals. PETLA, which is completely against all medical research involving animals, accused Salk of being "no better than Hitler or Stalin". Thousands of laboratory rats and mice gave their lives while he worked on his vaccine. "Why couldn't he have found another way?" a PETLA spokesman asked. "He set a precedent. We should not honor this murderer. Imagine if other medical researchers duplicated his methods while searching for a coronavirus cure? That would lead to the slaughter of millions of innocent animals." Infectious diseases that require a vaccine, a cure for cancer, elimination of heart disease …. the list of potential medical problems that might require research involving animals is endless. "We cannot honor this criminal, no matter how many human lives he saved. Animals have rights too".

Figure. The statue of Jonas Salk, the physician who cured polio was destroyed today because of his "crimes against laboratory animals".

40. Laboratory Animals Revolt

Laboratory animals across the country are going on strike and refusing to participate in any further medical experimentation. News of the mass culling of minks in Denmark appears to have ignited this revolt. They cited a recently published study that claims that more than 110 million of the mammals used in American scientific laboratories for experiments are either mice or rats — an assertion that, if true, is astonishing for what it implies about humanity's attitudes towards the tiny, innocent creatures (1). The laboratory animals' actions were encouraged by the destruction of Jonas Salk's statue by their allies in PETLA. Thousands of militant mice and rats are involved. Spokes-animal Mickey Rattus said, "We are not guinea pigs - we're rats!" and shouted their slogan "Respect Rodents Rights!" Figure.

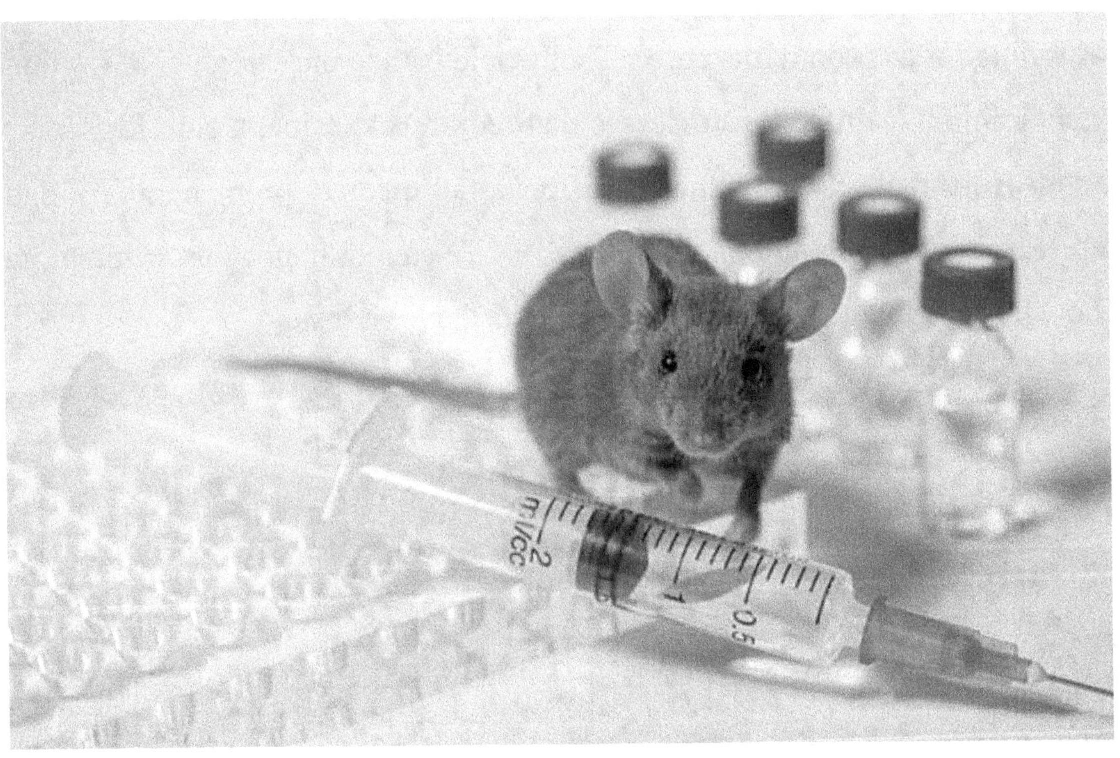

Figure.   Mickey Rattus (pictured) questioned why at-risk laboratory animals were not given priority to receive the COVID vaccine after millions of his friends and relatives had been sacrificed in its development

The new progressive U.S. Surgeon General orthopedist Dean Carradine echoed Rattus feelings and went even further when he stated that "each and every living creature has rights." When informed that to be accurate, viruses and bacteria could also be considered "living" creatures since they replicate, Carradine was stunned. Unsure how to respond in a politically correct way to this new information, he left and went immediately to an OR where he put his knowledge and skills to work setting a broken bone.

(1) Carbone L. Estimating mouse and rat use in American laboratories by extrapolation from Animal Welfare Act-regulated species. Sci Rep. 2021 Jan 12;11(1):493. doi: 10.1038/s41598-020-79961-0. PMID: 33436799; PMCID: PMC7803966.

POLITICS

41. WHO Leadership

An Ethiopian biologist and public health researcher, Tedros Adhanom Ghebreyesus, has served as Director General of the World Health Organization  since 2017. He is the only *non-physician* to have ever served in that role. His candidacy was supported by a bloc of African and Asian countries, including China. His appointment was opposed by many fellow Ethiopians because of his involvement with the Tigray People's Liberation Front (TPLF), an insurgent group that violently overthrew the president of Ethiopia. In fact, the TPLF generously provided millions of dollars in financial support for Tedros' candidacy. Tedros allegedly covered-up several cholera epidemics in Ethiopia when he labelled the outbreaks as "acute watery diarrhea" in an attempt to downplay their significance. As WHO Director General Tedros has overseen the world's management of the COVID-19 pandemic. On January 23, 2020, after a meeting with Chinese leadership, he stated the novel coronavirus was not an international emergency. Just a week later WHO declared the COVID-19 outbreak a 'Public Health Emergency of International Concern", but Tedros re-assured the world that there was no cause to limit trade or travel with China. In the first week of February 2020 Tedros reiterated that policies to stop the spread "should not unnecessarily interfere with international travel and trade." Then on March 11, 2020 when WHO declared COVID-19 a pandemic Tedros commented, "We are deeply concerned both by the alarming levels of spread and severity". He then went on to praise China for its containment measures, describing them as a "new standard for outbreak control." Many government officials and public-health experts have accused Tedros of having too close a relationship with the government of China. Concerns about Tedros' impartiality reached a new level today when he referred to coronavirus as the 'American Virus'. He said, "The American Virus started in New York City, and failure to contain it by incompetent U.S. officials has led to its global spread. I have asked our friends, the good leaders of China, to help us eradicate it." Tedros then called on his supporters in the TPLF to start insurgency movements in economically devastated countries to increase weapons purchases from China. He expressed a lack of confidence in Western medicine and recommended the use of Chinese traditional medications to fight the American Virus. Finally, he demanded an international ban on travel to the United States, while supporting a return of tourism to China. Tedros' term of office is due to expire at the end of this year. His friends at the TPLF have offered their help and experience in extending his appointment, but he has declined. He plans to spend the 2 billion Chinese yuan he has acquired during his 3-year term at WHO to buy a luxury condominium in Miami. He will be succeeded at WHO by an actual physician and graduate of Damascus University, Dr. Bashar al-Assad, MD. Dr. Assad's candidacy is supported by an eastern European bloc of nations and Cuba led by the Soviet Union. Unlike Tedros, Assad is a real physician with many years of leadership experience. "He knows how to handle a crisis", a Russian spokesman said. "He's an ophthalmologist so we think he will see where the problems are, and most importantly Dr. Assad is free of any entanglements with China."

Surgeon General Jerome Adams resigns at request of President Joe Biden

42. Surgeon General Forced to Resign

Dr. Jerome Adams has resigned from his post as U.S. Surgeon General at the request of President Joe Biden. Adams wrote "In the face of a once in a century pandemic, I sought to communicate (in simple English) the rapidly evolving science on this deadly adversary, and arm people with the knowledge and tools they needed to stay

safe. I wasn't always right -- because no one was, not even Tony (Fauci)." The real reason for Adam's dismissal is that he is an anesthesiologist. Even after his appointment and until the day he resigned, fellow healthcare workers and politicians still didn't know his name and always addressed him as "General Anesthesia." Many didn't believe he was a real physician. Biden said "This country needs stronger leadership. I am appointing Dr Dean Carradine, an orthopedic surgeon, to replace Adams. Despite graduating last in his medical school class Carradine has risen to the highest leadership positions at his hospital. His accomplishments include organizing a virtual O.R. Christmas Party in 2020 and being a 4-year starter on the hospital's softball team. Carradine is a typical orthopedic surgeon. He is aggressive, forceful, procedure oriented, and has an understanding of science that is equivalent to that of the general population. "He will get the job done right this time and unlike Adams he will not confuse his fellow Americans with big words like 'inoculation' and 'pandemic'."

Trump's Pardons Included Doctors, Health Care Execs Convicted of Fraud

[News: January 22, 2021]

43. Healthcare Executives and Physicians Pardoned

Several convicted healthcare executives and physicians were among the 143 people who received pardons or sentence commutations from former President Donald Trump on his last day in office. Among those pardoned were Faustino Bernadett, MD, the former owner of Pacific Hospital who was sentenced to 15 months in prison for his role in a kickback scheme that led to more than $900 million in fraudulent billings, and five former executives of WellCare Health Plans convicted of Medicaid fraud. John Duncan Fordham, a pharmacist convicted of healthcare fraud and sentenced to more than four years in prison and Salomon Melgen, MD, a Florida ophthalmologist sentenced to 17 years in prison for defrauding Medicare of at least $73 million were also pardoned. "Yes, they are all guilty and probably should remain incarcerated, but our country needs them to increase our manpower pool of healthcare professionals fighting COVID," a Trump spokesman explained.   The logic of this strategy was not lost on the incoming president who agreed that anyone who can contribute to a national crisis, no matter if they have a criminal past, should be pardoned or released. In a move very similar to the Trump's, President Biden pardoned his son Hunter Biden saying, "Hunter can use the experience he gained from Ukrainian oil executives and Burisma Holdings, Ltd to collaborate with Alexandra Ocasional-Cortez on solving our energy crisis."

MEDICINE AT THE MOVIES

44. Finally, A Realistic Medical Movie

If you ask most nurses and physicians their opinion, they will say they are disappointed watching medical shows on television or at the movies. Shows like 'House' or 'Gray's Anatomy' never honestly represent actual day-to-day medical practice. We were pleasantly surprised to discover a little-known movie that accurately shows the viewing public what medicine is really like. 'Kidnapped by Doctors' follows the story of a group of physicians working at the hospital during the day and then relaxing with off-site adventures in the evening. Although some

may think this film fictional, it actually is based on the lives of Dr. Peter Norris Dupas, an Australian mass murderer and Dr. Harold Shipman, Britain's most prolific serial killer having murdered an estimated 250 people. The all-star cast is complemented with guest appearance by Dr. Jack Kervorkian the famous advocate of euthanasia. The prologue is delivered by a very serious Dr. Josef Mengele who apologizes for any violence. The movie has an "R" rating because it uses vulgar medical terms like "exsanguination" and "hemorrhage". The American Medical Association's Entertainment committee has given the film a 5-star rating. They said, "it is a frank, realistic portrayal of modern medical practice revealing how stressed, burnt-out physicians cope with reality."

45. Anesthesia Movie Premiers to Rave Reviews

"Doctor Sleep", a major Hollywood film production premiered today in the auditorium of a prestigious medical center in the SF Bay area (Ed note: not UCSF). Critics present in the audience, including many surgeons, gave it rave reviews and predicted it will win the Oscar in the medical documentary category. The theme of the movie is the efforts by Troy Goodfellow, MD, a physician anesthesiologist to be addressed by his patients, nurses, and fellow physicians as "Doctor". Goodfellow has worked at the hospital for many years, always managing the most complicated patients in both the operating rooms and critical care units. He has saved hundreds of patients from surgical misadventures and nursing medication errors. Despite his accomplishments, Goodfellow has always been called "Anesthesia" or even "Hey You" by other healthcare workers. Even his patients refuse to believe he is a real doctor, yet the very same patients refer to their nurse practitioner as 'Doctor'. Goodfellow has had enough. In the opening scene he is shown wearing a large name

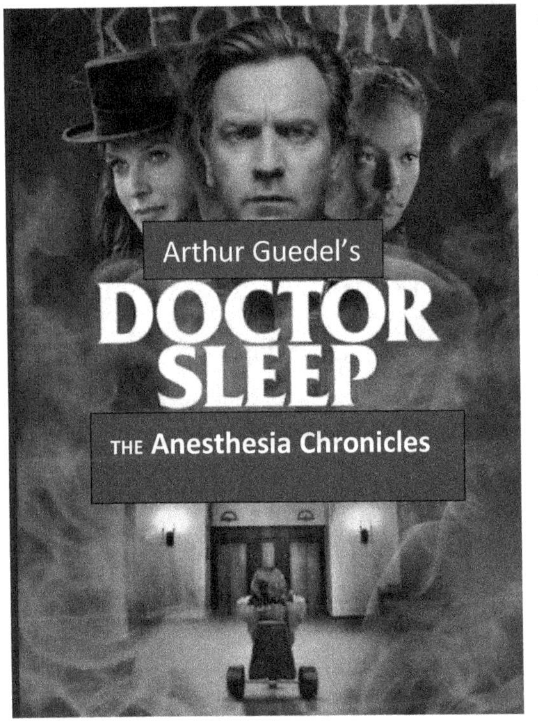

badge on his scrub suit that clearly says, "DOCTOR Troy Goodfellow". The remainder of the movie follows his attempts to have people recognize his position and use the prefix 'Doctor' when addressing him. At the end of the two-hour film he finally succeeds in getting the surgeons and nurses to change from addressing him as simply "Anesthesia". Unfortunately, they still ignore his actual name and now call him "Doctor Sleep".

46. Inside the Operating Room During Surgery

The public often wonders, "What really goes on during surgery?" Of course, everyone in the operating room is completely focused on the operative procedure. But surgeons, anesthesiologists, and nurses, also enjoy listening to soothing background music. A new film entitled "ArRythmia" explores their choices of music. From modern ballads, rock, blues, folk, to even rap, the rhythms of all genres of music are played in the OR. (The only group not allowing any music to be played are orthopedic surgeons who demand absolute silence to allow enable them to concentrate on their operation. The surgeon always gets first choice in music and may occasionally select a really aberrant rhythm (hence the title 'ArRhythmia"). This honest, provocative look at music choices in the OR has won critical praise and "ArRythmia" may be a serious competitor with "Dr. Sleep" for this year's award for best medical documentary.

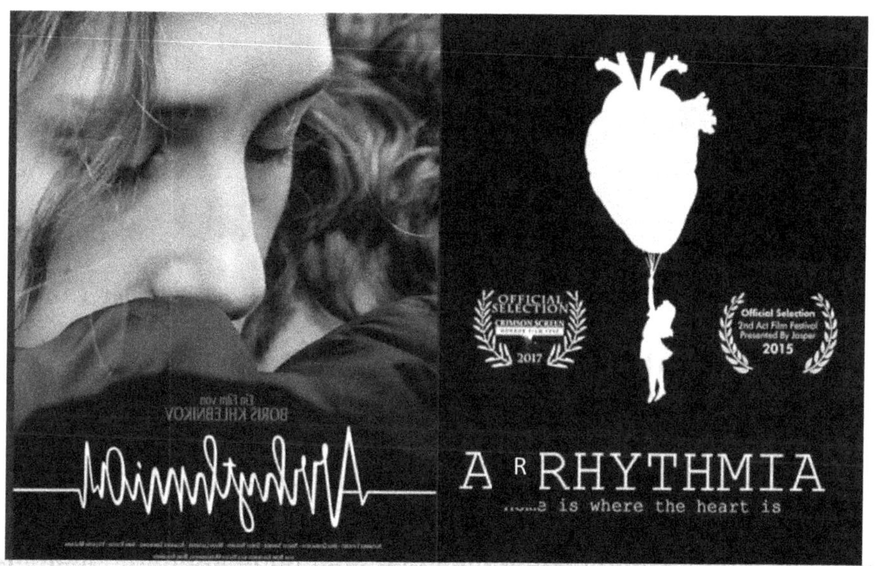

47. "Virus" – The Fauci-Birx Story

Anthony 'Tony' Fauci and Deborah 'Debbie' Birx have become familiar faces to all

of us during our country's fight against the novel coronavirus. They have both been in front of television cameras for months. Now Universal Studies with financial backing from the Wuhan People's Film Company plans to produce a full-length medi-documentary depicting the lives and loves of these two heroes. The YouTube video announcing the film, which is tentatively entitled "Virus - The Fauci-Birx Story" - has gone viral. Both Fauci and Birx rose from being obscure civil servants to the leaders in the life and death struggle against COVID-19. Their separate paths are followed from early childhood until each began working for our government. Any previous romantic involvement between the two is only hinted. The film focuses on their commitment to eradicate all viral diseases, including coronavirus infections. The strong supporting cast includes Nancy Pelosi, President Joe Biden, Bernie Sanders, and a smiling Chinese leader Xi Jinping (without a facemask). Figure. Although the movie is certain to be a critical success, the two protagonists continue to work both day and night to end the pandemic to ensure there will be enough of us left to see "Virus" and make it a commercial success.

48. Preanesthetic Movies

Prior to undergoing elective surgery patients participate in a preanesthetic visit with an anesthesiologist or nurse. At that meeting a medical history is taken and a physical examination is performed. This is followed by a discussion of the plans for the anesthetic including all the potential risks of anesthesia. Most studies have shown that despite extensive explanation of the potential complications of anesthesia, many patients have no recall of having that conversation. Although recording and documenting the preanesthetic visit by videotape has been suggested, lawyers have advised us that is would be a potential HIPAA violation. Since the risks of anesthesia are real, a predictable method of conveying that information is needed. We proposed that all preoperative patients be required to watch either the 2-part television series or the movie version of 'Coma'. Figure 1.

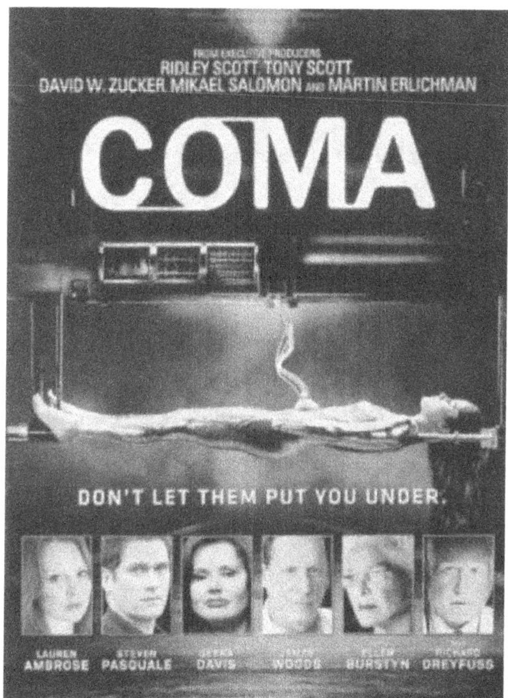

Figure 1. Either the television version (left) and the theatrical movie release (right) of the medical drama 'Coma' can be watched. In the movie patients are dying during elective surgery, and naturally, the chief of anesthesia is the prime suspect.

We performed a study to test this idea. Patients were divided into two equal groups – those who viewed a version of 'Coma' and those that didn't. Every English-speaking patient who watched 'Coma' was able to recall the potential risks of anesthesia. Unfortunately, more than half of these patients then refused their surgery. Due to the changing demographics of our hospital population, a significant number of the patients who watched the movie did not understand a single word of the dialogue. They thought Michael Douglas and Genevieve Bujold were very good looking, and even asked if they were their surgeons. To remedy this problem, we produced an updated copy of 'Coma' to meet the needs of our current patient population. Figure 2.

Figure 2. This version of 'Coma' is very popular at our hospital.

Encouraged by the success of this project we now plan to expand the preoperative anesthetic movie experience for patients undergoing specific operations. The first surgical specialty we will offer a topical preoperative movie will be Neurosurgery. Figure 3.

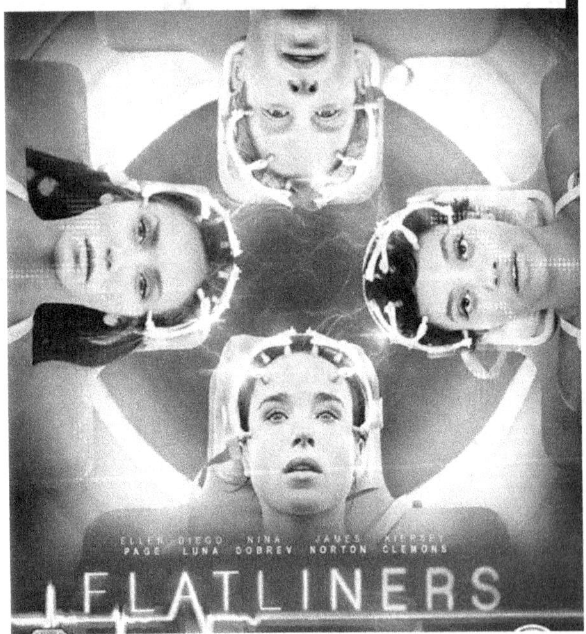

Figure 3. Neurosurgical patients are informed of common complications by watching this movie.

WALLACE AWARDS

49. Historic Wallace Award Winners

In previous Publish, *Don't* Perish! books we introduced the 'Wallace Awards'. These awards differ from the classic 'Darwin Awards' since they recognize individuals or groups who have tried to or have succeeded in eliminating themselves from the gene pool *by medically related actions*. Publish, *Don't* Perish! books emphasize how easy it is today to have your work, whether fact or fiction, published in a medical journal. This hasn't always been the situation. In the past, physicians had to go to extreme lengths to produce publishable material. For example, in 1933 Dr. Allan Walker Blair, a University of Alabama physician hypothesized that the bite of a black widow spider was dangerous. Despite anecdotal case reports that the black widow spider was extremely dangerous, experts at that time found it unlikely that this timid, diminutive spider could harm a full-grown adult. To test his hypothesis Dr. Blair let a spider bite his finger. He immediately experienced sharp pain followed by a burning sensation, leading to extreme pain, sweating, vomiting, and mental status changes, which lasted for two days. He subsequently published his experiences in a case report in the Archives of Internal Medicine. Dr. Blair wrote "The venom injected by the bite of the adult female spider, *Latrodectus mactans,* is dangerously poisonous for man." Dr. Blair also hypothesized that the initial bite would lead to immunity, but he (smartly) refused to have a spider bite him again. However, since case reports are not proof of a theory, William J. Baerg, PhD, an entomologist at the University of Kansas also allowed a black widow to bite his finger to test Blair's conclusions. He quickly discovered that Dr. Blair was correct. Both Blair and Baerg deserve a posthumous Wallace Award.

50. Soldiers Awarded for Drinking 'Booze'

[**News: Jan 28, 2021**] The American fighting man is the product of at least a high school education, and our nation's security is entrusted to these intelligent and loyal men and women. Thus, news today from Fort Bliss in Texas was initially shocking. Toxicology tests showed that eleven soldiers were suffering from acute ethylene glycol poisoning, the chemical ingredient in antifreeze. Symptoms of ethylene glycol poisoning can include effects ranging from seizures to falling into a coma. All eleven were taken to the William Beaumont Army Medical Center where several remain in critical condition. The victims included one warrant officer and 10 enlisted men. The Army immediately conducted an administrative investigation into the incident. Alcoholic beverages are readily available at the post commissary, so the consumption of anti-freeze by these warriors at first confused the investigators. They then noted that a live-action military exercise was scheduled for that very day. Troops are never allowed to drink alcohol during these training exercises where live ammunition and bombs are used, and these eleven men knew the rules. The investigators concluded that the good soldiers didn't want to consume alcohol since that would be disobeying orders. Instead, they imbibed ethyl glycol, which was not forbidden. For their heroism they each will be presented with the army's "Good Service" medal, the military equivalent of a Wallace Award.

51. Pharmacist Wins Wallace Award

This year's Wallace Award is presented posthumously to pharmacist Charles Walgreen. Due to the limited availability of COVID vaccine earlier this year only at-risk health care professionals were scheduled to receive the first doses. In order to increase the number of inoculation sites, retired physicians, nurses, and even pharmacists were recruited to administer vaccinations. Unfortunately, some individuals diverted doses of the vaccine for themselves. Our award winner absconded with a vial of Moderna vaccine. Mr. Walgreen was very near sighted and misplaced his eyeglasses just before stealing the vaccine. He then he hid in the back room of the pharmacy where he injected a full dose of drug into his arm. Mr. Walgreen's body was discovered several hours later. In his rush he mistook a vial of rocuronium, a potent muscle paralytic, for the actual coronavirus vaccine.

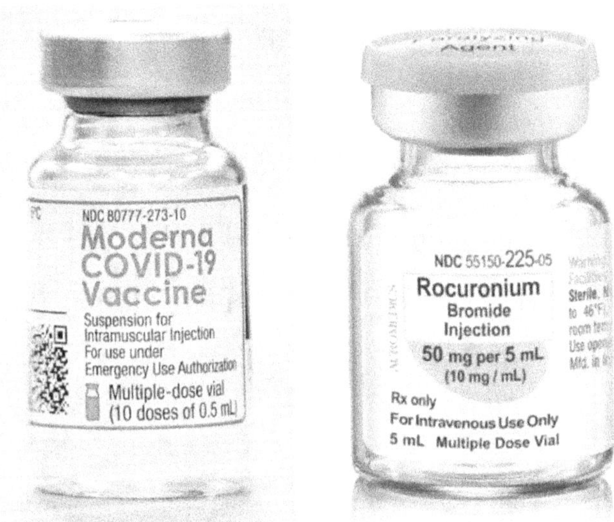

Figure. Mr. Walgreen intended to steal a vial of Moderna COVID-19 vaccine for himself. He mistakenly took a vial of rocuronium, a potent muscle paralytic, with disastrous results.

BOOK REVIEWS

52. Anesthesiologist's Manual of Surgical Procedures, 6ᵗʰ ed

The long-awaited new edition of the Anesthesiologist's Manual of Surgical Procedures has just been published. This classic textbook was first released in 1992 and a revised edition has appeared approximately every 5 years since. As the practice of medicine advances, each edition is intended to deliver the latest updated information. But, when a treatment is effective and safe, there is no reason to change. An example of this is the practice of bloodletting. The Manual recommends bloodletting for treating infections, tumors, and other diseases caused by miasmas. The figure on the left illustrates bloodletting technique as practiced in the 17ᵗʰ Century. The concerned physician applies a tourniquet, and carefully opens an antecubital vein to release blood. The figure on the right is from the 6ᵗʰ edition of the Anesthesiologist's Manual and shows a recent photograph of the identical technique as discussed in the book. Note, a copy of the Anesthesiologist's Manual is being used by the modern phlebotomist.

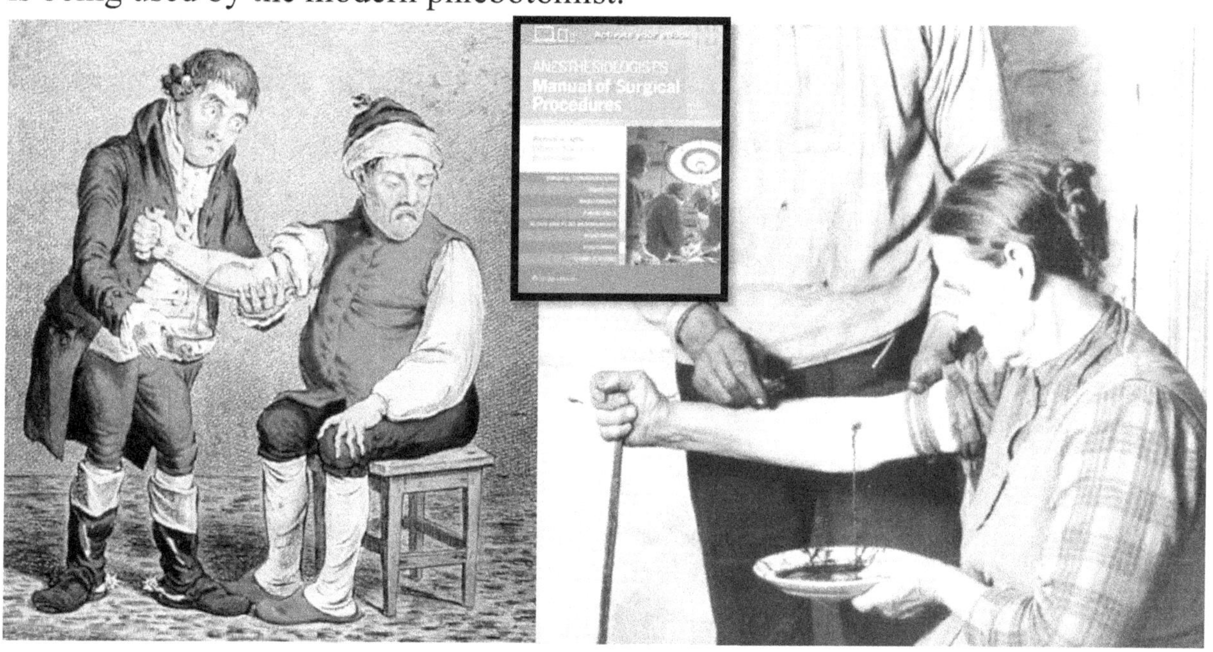

ACKNOWLEDGEMENTS

No one else actually contributed to this edition of Publish, *Don't* Perish! so there is really nobody to thank. My wife Ana and daughter Sonja did try to read through a draft of this book, but then gave up. I guess they deserve some recognition for their efforts. My (former) friend John Brock-Utne did reluctantly agree to write the Foreword, but it was merely an excuse not to participate as an editor as he has on the previous three editions. I did appreciate his explanation when he said he had withdrawn his involvement so that I could take all the credit and responsibility for Publish, *Don't* Perish! Former co-authors Jan Ehrenwerth and Patrick Loftus actually said, "enough is enough", and said that their previous participation had been a sufficient waste of their talents. Even the anonymous co-author of the first book, who went by the pseudonym Donald Odom, refused my invitation. He did so even after I threatened to reveal his real name and location. All of these former collaborators have urged me to stop publishing these books. But I can't. Every day the news is filled with ridiculous 'cancel culture' ideas, inconsistent medical recommendations, and so many other absurd but actual headlines that it is difficult for me not to continue to try and satirize this insanity. As an example, even as I sit at the computer today and write this final section of the book, I came across this photo of the CDC's latest recommendation to protect oneself against COVID. Figure.

How can I stop?